mass. murder.

Younger Charles Robbins

Published by Adjar, LLC 2023
Younger Robbins: Member Adjar, LLC
Logo design: Erin Cathcart

Cover art by:
Chris Mott
@chrismottart

ISBN: 979-8-218-10086-5

Thank You

Massachusetts, 1954

The bomber-sight hood emblem affixed to my heap stands cocked to the right, luring me to nudge the wheel off the rutted asphalt into the darkness waiting on the highway's edge. White knuckles.

The wheel wracks my bones and does a whole helluva lot better keeping me awake than the dirt-water coffee I got back before civilization cut off and the lights of Boston twinkled into memory.

Usually, I'd appreciate a country drive. Fresh air, green grass, a silly blonde or two weighing down the backseat, the road wet with the mid-of-night clamminess that slicks hands and dews the prude flower petal wrapped up delicately in the gleam of the moon. I would come up here a lot right after I got stateside. When the noise of the city got to be too much. The screech of a trolley or a bum carburetor could bring you back no problem.

White-hot fear of life and death in an instant. Sweat or piss or blood. Incitement in the first degree. Somewhere you've never been. Someone you never knew. The snow clings to the hedgerows with terminal faith. Shading reality, obscuring the full metal truth lying in wait not inches away.

Best to forget it.

Keep going north and you'll be hard pressed to find a place to eat, let alone a care to give. Somewhere around where the lakes meet the clouds and time escapes reckoning, the Ammonoosuc escapes Mt. Washington, flowing south until converging with the Connecticut River to feed the greater good. From that same tributary run many other veins pumping with the life-artery of the land. The same waters that surged to serve the Abenaki and the Danish now run concurrent with my own course.

I crossed the bridge into town, parked the heap, lit up and sat waiting for Nancy Brighton. Nancy was a nice girl and she needed help. I was an amiable guy and more than happy to invest my time in Nancy's plight—or rather that of her brother: Donnie Brighton, a local boy, college-dropout, Naval reserves kind of character turned working man then ladies' man. He was soon a wanted man after coming too close to the wire with the wife of a workplace chum. The next anyone saw of said chum, he's floating in the Merrimack shot twice. The wife gets a hefty sentence. And Donnie? Sounds like now he's got the old ants pants 'cause Nancy's worried and he's nowhere to be found. The local Finest would surely be happy to have him go the way of the wind and never give the whole matter second thought.

Nancy, on the other hand, is nowhere to be found.

I'm starting to wonder whether it's a better bet to sleep in the heap or turn and burn, trying to make it back to the city before morning.

It was no small count that the pockets of Uncle Sam had run dry around the same time everybody decided they could handle their personal matters without my help.

Chin up.

That's what I told Vicky when I told her we'd have to stop the milk delivery and start conserving gasoline, then rethink the office lease. After that I could peddle my services door-to-door:

Pardon me, ma'am. Joe Burke Private Investigator. Any missing persons in the house today? A drug dealer upstairs or kidnapper in the basement? I've got a reasonable day rate and no retainer. If you like, you could even strap a saddle on me, and we'll go run the errands.

When I came around the corner of the main street I noticed someone nosing around the Buick. I hung back and watched while they messed with the wiper blade, glanced around and took off. I went and got what was a note stuck to the windshield.

please excuse my late timing
not good to speak tonight
meet here tomorrow same time
will reimburse completely for expenses
  -N

I crumpled the note.
"Just fine."

I caught up without much trouble, as Nancy entered a driveway a couple neighborhoods out of downtown. She passed a wind-worn Victorian which had attained the state of forlorn dustiness buildings get when no longer possessed. In the yard behind the main home was a single-story cottage. The lights in the cottage blinked on.

I hunkered down by one of the windows and poked my nose up over the window sill. Nancy held a phone to her ear.

She appeared to be alone.

Some clothes hung near a wood-burning stove. Some books, mostly magazines were spread around on a night table near an old four-poster that took up most of the room.

When Nancy came close to the window I could hear the muffled sound of her voice but not well enough to make out any details. When she turned away I went to the front door and tested the handle, slowly. The door gave and I slipped in. Nancy hung up and turned with a start.

"What do you think this is?" Nancy faced me.

"Who was that on the phone?"

"What matter is it of yours?"

"Some, I'd bet."

We waited.

"So you're Burke?" finally.

I fished a business card and credentials from the wallet in my jacket pocket. I showed her the credentials and handed her the card. Jet-black hair falling over gentle blue eyes. I offered her a smoke and she accepted, allowing me to light it before I lit my own. The struck match showed the concern on her face. When the flare died, the warm orange glow of the cottage softened all things, including my tone.

"Want to tell me who was on the phone, now?"

"My mother. She's so concerned lately it makes me on edge. I don't know what I was thinking. You are who you are... I suppose. I was only worried."

I smoked.

"There's no chance you were followed?"

"By who?"

I almost laughed, "Before I saw you I was starting to think I was the only one alive in the whole town."

"It's the middle of the night you know."

"You don't have to tell me," I snipped.

"I'm sorry. I didn't mean anything by it. I'm tired. I guess I'm the one who forgot the time." She took her story over to the bed and slumped on the edge with one leg crossed over the other at the knee. "Ever since this whole business with Donnie started I've been on edge. Ma's in no shape to hear about any of this. After daddy passed last year she hasn't been the same and she loves Donnie so much."

"And now you're thinking that you and your brother might be deserving of some reparations? Thought a washed-up joker from the city could come up here and do your digging for you?"

"No," she protested.

"Find some dirt the local boys didn't want to deal with and land a defamation suit against the state?"

"No." She stood, stubbing out the butt.

"Then what is it! What the hell are you into and why'd you drag me up here in the middle of the night? Tell me the truth, 'cause I ain't got time for the rest." She didn't protest this time, didn't move a muscle, but her eyes glazed over with the crystal sheen of tears to come. I was in resplendent form. The stick I forgot in my hand burned my fingers before going out.

all the shit that's fit to print

"Donnie is missing," she finally breathed.

By the time I heard Nancy's whole story, the sun was threatening over the tree line. Nancy offered me a spot to crash which I didn't accept. She was nervous, that was easy to see. Her brother Donnie was gone. Whatever gave him the spooks, Nancy didn't know or was doing a good job of pretending. Though deeply involved with the married woman in the romantic sense, Donnie hadn't done any jail time and was free to do as he'd pleased.

I made it back to the Buick in the full light of morning and moved the heap to a less conspicuous locale. I walked back to the center of town looking for a place to eat and got steak and eggs at a diner, pounded down a cup of dirt-water and sat over a second, ruminating. The girl brought the bill and I paid out of pocket. So far I passed on taking any dough from old Nance. With a fairly drawn-out trial recently closed, I can only imagine there wasn't much cash to go around.

Before leaving I dialed my answering service from the

phone in the wall and got a couple of looks from some of my fellow patrons while doing so. Likely the locals were sore on newcomers after having the murder trial circus pass through. I finished up without any messages to hear and took off.

In the basement of the public library I found some newspapers from several weeks past. About every day there was an article published related to the murder. Some of the stuff I had seen covered in the Boston papers. Some of it was more local junk stories trying to get interviews with Donnie's mother, questions of his integrity, opinions on his appearance and fortitude. All the important stuff that news is made of.

It struck me as odd that Donnie escaped the murder implications so easily. A more recent article made the whole story much more clear.

Cliff Mason Jr., Navy veteran, father of three, thirty-one years old at his time of death at the hands of Elizabeth Mason, his wife. Not long before Cliff's body was hauled out of the Merrimack and identified, Elizabeth filed for divorce claiming that Cliff was unstable, unfaithful, and violent. A lot of time that was true, a husband comes home after having a few rips and gives the missus the regular pop only this time she can't stand it, and she lets him have it. Usually, she uses the guy's own gun from out of the hall closet. Sad, but true and easy for all involved. Open and shut—the wife does some time, but it's light 'cause everyone knows the guy would have probably killed her eventually. Double that with kids involved.

That's how Elizabeth's case was wrapped up, too. With Cliff

tossed over the bridge out of town, unable to tell his side of the story, the only thing to go on were the statements Elizabeth made to the local DA who made fast work of the whole thing. Before you know it, justice had been served, and Elizabeth was behind bars.

More reading and now Donnie's involved. He worked with Cliff building glass bulbs, and the two became pals. Soon after, Donnie reportedly became pals with Elizabeth too.

In the trial, Donnie reveals that Elizabeth is not the only woman he's been seeing, he's willing to admit all the nights he spent with Elizabeth, but on the night of the murder, according to Donnie's own testimony, he was out with Judith Whitlock another friend with similar interests. There were a lot more ancillary details and fancy writing to sift through but no more real information to be had. I left the library and crossed the street to the town hall to take a look at the property maps near Nancy's place.

Turns out the place she's staying is owned by something called Wainsforth, Miller & Co., probably a holding company or insurance agency. None of the previous owners seemed to have any relation to Nancy Brighton and its unlikely that her mother would have owned the place under a maiden name. Most likely the place was foreclosed on when the boom of wartime had passed and now the local caretaker rents out the back house to visitors and passers-through.

When I got to the heap it was no place to be found.

I double-checked my memory and was sure that I owned a car, sure that I drove one, and almost positive I parked it right where I was. I lit up and watched a patrol car turn into the dirt lot, kicking up dust until it got next to me.

The window rolled down.

"Afternoon, boys. You my ride?" I leaned in to get a look at the two uniformed officers: young guy riding shotgun and an older guy, the salt, at the wheel.

"Get in. You want your car don't ya?" barked the driver.

"Depends on the forecast. I was considering walking back to Boston."

"You're gonna be skidding back on your ass unless you quit your yapping and get in," said the driver.

I considered the image for a moment then got in.

Sitting in back with my knees up to my chin I got the daytime tour of the town, same as at night, only with color. Lots of folks out shopping and eating, keeping the community afloat with their savings. The mills at the falls had long been surpassed by larger operations and the auto industry never really caught on here though they tried. Children of farmers grown up sweeping rejected nails off the manufacturing floor and enlisting in the Navy after that. Some with ambition made a struggling commute into the city for a high-paying job or at least the promise of that. Others ventured north and west in search of new roots and untilled earth, but most stayed right here hemmed in by river and sea, transitioned from the reserve forces of the wartime behemoth to the working force. Taking advantage of the local manufacturers who like the men were changing.

Across the entire country the metal of bullets had been appropriated back into children's toys. The Chrysler sedan rolled out instead of the light tank M5 and the bulbs in the spotlights that lit the underbellies of foreign planes running airstrikes on distant American bases now illuminated the silvery stardust of the hometown movie screen.

Bulbs handcrafted by Cliff Mason and Donnie Brighton.

The police station wasn't far from the center of town. We made it there without conversation. When we arrived my chauffeurs escorted me past receiving, booking, holding—all my favorite stomping grounds—and right straight back to the man in charge.

Captain Hansen didn't wear any suit coat. He had his sleeves rolled up below his elbows, the size of his arms wouldn't allow for any higher. He opened a window and pulled half a cigar out of a drawer in his desk. He lit the burnt end with a match, shook the match until it was extinguished and tossed it out the window. He sat at his desk puffing at his cigar with not much of a look on his face. He was older, balding and tired-looking.

"Have a seat there," he said, gesturing with his hand to the chair facing him. "You can smoke in here if you like."

"I'm all out. Unless you want to share."

"Who are you? What are you doing here?"

"I came in for the day. I'm thinking of buying a summer place. You know, get away from it all."

"I was hoping you were gonna be different than all the others. Wisecracks and billfolds from you jokers, that's all I get. Let's have the credentials."

I pulled out my auto license, a license permitting me to practice as a private investigator, and business card with the office numbers, phone, and street.

"Won't be needing your library card. We already know you can get in there. Don't worry, Burke. I don't mean nothing by it. That's my own way of cracking wise—don't need a license to do that."

"Got me." I put my hands up, palms facing him.

"That covers who you are. And I already reckon plain enough what brings you here so I'm gonna go ahead and say it right up front. I'm gonna have the boys take you to your car at the impound lot. You can pick it up free of charge, and then you can head back home."

"I'll need time to grab a bite and some smokes–"

"Your vehicle was parked on Franklin since halfway through the night and on the bluffs near the park since morning. I don't know where you were in between and I don't want to. You had a meal at Eddie's Diner. I know that. You've seen our historic buildings and pleasant community and now I welcome you to get out."

I started to open my mouth but didn't stand a chance.

"There's a gas station after the bridge out of town. You can get your cigarettes there or in Cincinnati for all I care."

The vibrant colors of the world interspersed by black and rose every time I closed my eyes. Glorious moments of peace lasting only as long as it took to draw the lids back up. Each repetition taking more time than the last until I was lost in the half-waking dream world of unrest. The midday warmed my face through the gaps of late spring greenery. The rains had come and everything that grows showed appreciation by reaching toward the sky, pistils toward the sun, leaves fanning out to absorb the nutrient rays. When we got to the impound lot the young cop got out and opened the back door of the cruiser.

"You heard the Captain, now do as you're told," he had been waiting to say.

I reached for a smoke and remembered I was still out.

"Got a smoke?" he about turned purple.

"I don't have squat for the likes of you. Now do as you're told and scram," he called out as I brushed past him. "And don't get any smart ideas. We'll be following you to the city limits!"

"Just fine."

My buddies did as they promised, staying close to my bumper the whole way out of town. At this time of day I could make it back to Boston before sunset without stopping on the way. I could easily catch ten or twelve hours of sleep and make it back to the office in time to get my belongings before they changed the locks. For all I know there was a new message on the answering service begging of my skill-set for easy work and a quick payoff. None of this down-home, tight-lipped, appearance-keeping.

Give me a dope-fiend grandson run off to the Hamptons who needs persuading to return to Cambridge, or a trick with the scoop on a murder who needs protection from the guilty party before she can dish. That's bread and butter. This small-town stuff is bird seed. So a guy fools around with four or five guy's wives and has to stick his head in the sand for a while.

Happens every day some places.

People get used to covering things up and others get used to the cover so that they can convince others it's truth. Somewhere the matter of truth becomes so meaningless that whatever happened has been lost and the parties involved can all go on with their election, or promotion, or whatever it is that the elite members of upstanding society value above things like truth and consequence.

I went south out of Amesbury, passing under the new, six-lane expressway. I crossed the bridge out of town with the boys in my rearview still following close behind. I pulled into the service station after the bridge and killed the ignition. The boys pulled the cruiser over to the side of the road and waited while I pumped gas and went inside the station to pay.

When I returned with a fresh pack of smokes they were still there. I lit up and waved a friendly so-long to the cruiser before getting inside the Buick and driving off. I followed the cut of the river a few miles away toward the coast.

The way things felt, Donnie seemed more like a runaway than a target. Sure his case was funny, but so is life. A guy gets embarrassed or ashamed, he hides away, changes his name, gets a new job, and starts making a new existence.

The cops, even Hansen, all had a mouse in their teeth squeaking to get out. The feeling was spread throughout the whole town. Probably why Nancy was on edge. It's not that everyone's sick of the exposure so much as that they're all holding onto something that hasn't been exposed yet. The limits had been pushed when the murder surfaced and it's been pressing right on everyone's forehead ever since. I got into Seabrook before too late in the day, but the seaside temperature had already begun to drop.

A few miles into the town I came across a used car dealer. About a half hour and a lot of glad-handing later I left as the proud new owner of a '48 Chevy. The used car hustler recognized the Buick as a steal of a trade-in, bent hood mount and all. He put four hundred cash in my hand on top of the pink for the Chevy. It caused me a great pain to part with the heap but the show must go on, and since the thing was barely too cramped to live in, I saluted my old friend in commemoration of time served as I drove off in the new old used Chevy. I cruised the coast feeling things out and found a seafood spot to have some clams with butter and potatoes and slaw and a couple of beers. I thought of having a third beer with cash burning a hole in my pocket but decided on coffee.

The all-glass front of the building created a panorama of the Atlantic Ocean roaring methodically, drawing the sand out as the tide moved in. To the hypnotized bystander the sea appeared to be consuming the earth and would take me with it if the waters were to beat at the stilts of the diner foundation, dissolving the pylons as it would the sand, the floor boards and benches and me next.

What the Chevy lacked in horsepower it made up for with drabness. We blended right into the middle-class evening, challenged by the lights of Main Street. Beyond that there was no affront to the night, which turned the sea into a new universe. I went south into Salisbury, cutting over the back roads to Nancy's from the opposite direction as before. I parked down the block when I got there and killed the lights.

No sign of anyone on the street or in the empty front house. I got out and walked back to the cottage which was dark and appeared empty. Having been successful once, I tried the knob and found the door unlocked. No secrets around here.

The inside of the cottage was how I remembered it. The stove had been used and there was a blouse or two around. Nothing peculiar. I picked up the phone, the line was clear.

The table was covered with writing paper, magazines, an ashtray, some letters. One, addressed care of Wainsforth, Miller & Co. was open, a bill for the rent. On the wall were some framed pictures: a woman wearing a fairly ornate dress could be seen sitting on a porch railing, smoking. Behind her, several women—much younger and more beautiful than she, but also not wearing such lavish attire—stood as though at attention. Sisters, or graduates at a finishing school? Another picture in a frame showed two men, one some years older, a commander it looked like. The other man wore rank, but it could not be distinguished. They stood side-by-side near the bow of an aircraft carrier. Wartime, or more likely shortly after based on their dress and decoration. They beamed proudly, chins pointing.

Some other knick-knacks and decorations hung around, all of which must have been the left-behinds of previous owners.

The door opened, and Nancy stepped in.

"Mr. Burke," she said. "I was beginning to think you weren't planning on coming back."

"I'm here."

"Do you have any news? Anything from Donnie?"

"Now hold it, kid. I've only decided to make a start and I'm already having a helluva time doing anything about it."

"How do you mean?"

"I met a few of the local police. You might have had the same pleasure with better luck than me."

"The whole department was there. What's his name?"

She had removed her overcoat leaving it on a hook near the door. She moved about the room, straightening up in a half-hearted way. She bent down to clean up the blouses on the floor and gave me quite a view of the one she had on. She floated over to the stove and I was blessed as she drew fresh water into a pot before extracting a brown bag from a nearby cupboard. She poured coffee beans into a grinder and the aroma filled the room at once. I could see the oil on the beans from the table where I sat. Soft fingers rolled down the worn paper bag, concealing again the hidden treasure in the cupboard before returning to the stove, spreading out over the smooth cast iron without touching, testing the heat. Nancy handled the grinder attentively, facing the stove. The lithe muscles of her neck and shoulders tensed as the beans changed form. She transferred the grounds to a press and filled it with boiling water. Pushed back her hair, breathing deep. I closed my eyes for what seemed like the first time in days and could feel Nancy exhale. When I opened my eyes the urn and two cups were on the tabletop. Nancy grasped the lid, depressing a screen into the boiling water slowly, methodically, allowing no single grain to surface to the top. As she moved, the beans darkened, steeped in the water, releasing sweet elixir.

"Hansen." I think I said at some point.

I drank Nancy's coffee.

"Have you filed a missing person's report for Donnie?"

"I haven't really spoken to anyone about anything. Only mother and you."

"Don't you want to find your brother? Don't you trust the cops?"

"You said yourself that you didn't get along with Mr. Hansen."

"Yeah, but that's in the script, kid. No self-respecting cop with a city and a job to think of wants anything to do with me. I might as well have a tattoo on my forehead and it's not a funny word. You on the other hand—it's not the same. When did you last talk to him?"

"I'm really not sure, sometime after Donnie was arrested. I saw Mr. Hansen at the courthouse during the trials but we never spoke. There was never a need."

I lit up, offering Nance a stick and poured us the last of the coffee.

"And after that, after you tried contacting Donnie and got nervous, you never followed up?"

"It's not as though I've ever done this before. I was scared."

"Then why bring me up here? Look Nance I want to help you—hell, at this point I'm invested—but if you can't be straight with me then I might as well beat it 'cause I've gone about as far as I can go."

She stood, went to the dresser, and came back with a notebook opened to a page marked by an envelope. She drew out a folded page from inside the already opened envelope and laid it out for me.

A man's handwriting.

My collar tightened as I read:

My Dearest Nancy,

I wanted to thank you for all the help that you have been in these recent weeks. Without your care and support I don't believe I could have made it this far. But I feel that now I have come to a point of a road that which when I began on it, seemed to go on un-ending. Now that ending seems to be right before me and I'm not sure I like the way it looks. I know as only blood could know that you believe me to be innocent of murder, and it's true! I am! But what I am guilty of will haunt me without respite every day I awaken in this town and so I've made the decision to go away. Please tell mother I'm sorry and tell her that I'm well. And please don't come after me. I'm sorry.

Love, Donnie

I lit another smoke to calm my nerves. The letter was clear and put me right smack in the middle of a goose hunt. Some people don't want to be found and Donnie was turning out to be one of them.

"I know what it looks like." Nancy read my mind.

"Sorry, Nance but I'm worried it's exactly what it looks like."

"But this isn't Donnie," she protested.

"He's young. He's understandably spooked. It makes sense. If you give him time, he'll end up coming back."

She unfolded another letter.

"This is a letter from Donnie to mother from a few months ago. Go ahead, read."

I did and she was right. The letter was signed by Donnie, but it was as though a different person had composed it, lacking the eloquent phrasing, filled with typos.

"It's different, that's for sure, but situations change a person. Your brother might have felt different when he wrote the last letter."

"My brother did not write this letter, Mr. Burke."

Right now, I was sympathizing with Hansen. This is exactly what happens when things get stirred up. Everyone starts seeing and feeling things that weren't there before.

"Couldn't you at least go around and ask," she continued, "I would do it myself but no one has wanted anything to do with me since I've been here."

"I don't know what makes you think I'll have any better luck."

"You have to, Mr. Burke. Please, can't you try?"

The last thing she brought out from the notebook was a light roll of bills.

"Fifty dollars," she said. It's all that mother and I can afford as an advance but I can have more wired from my aunt in Indiana. It may take one or two days but I can get more, I promise."

I took the cash and laid it out flat. I tore a blank page out Nancy's notebook and created an envelope for the cash. I got a letter of intent form from my wallet and had Nancy sign.

I took that and put it in the envelope with the cash and put the whole bundle inside my wallet.

"This is plenty for the time being. I'll poke around and if nothing comes up I'll return the cash before tomorrow night." I stood and started toward the door. Nancy followed. "I don't want you to hold out too great a hope for this, Nancy."

She grabbed onto me and wrapped her arms around my waist, her body up against mine, her head resting below my chin, cheek to my chest, ear to my heart.

"Thank you, Mr. Burke. You couldn't know how much it means to me. I've felt so lost until now. But with you here everything is finally starting to make some sense."

On my way back to the whip, despite the time of no-longer-night-but-morning, I decided now would be a good time to catch up on some much-needed sleep. A short drive would surely lead to a vacant room I could finally afford.

The pain in my shoulder was sudden and brief, right below the neck. I went down hard and without protest.

get me, copper

I woke up sitting in the driver's seat of the whip. The car was parked on the side of the road near the gas station past the bridge out of town. My head was swimming before I even moved. My eyes tugged on high tension wires. I sucked wind, and shuddered from down in my gut. Sweat formed on the back of my neck and on my forehead. I reached for the door handle, pressed the door open with my shoulder and tossed my insides on the dirt.

A search of my jacket revealed that my bankroll was still intact. Also inside my wallet was the paper envelope with Nancy's dough and signature. I fumbled turning the engine over, yanked the transmission into reverse and began to ease it backward along the side of the road. Whoever sapped me had done a damn fine job of it. Probably the old-salt patrol officer trying to teach the rookie. "Here's how you do it, son."

I rolled the Chevy backwards to the front of the gas station, spilled out through the open door, and did my best plodding along into the station without falling on my face.

I returned to the car where I sat and ate a few of the asprin I bought, washed down with a slug of rye whiskey. I took down a third of the bottle and put the rest away in the glove box. I got the car closed up and turned across the road going back into town. Though the liquor had done its job coating my nerves in a boozy sheet of armor, every jolt was another nail driven into my skull.

I parked at the curb in front of the precinct and headed up the stairs. I made my way to the open doors at the top, earning a few looks on the way. The desk sergeant hollered as I passed through the waiting area and into the bullpen, past the room full of on-duty officers the way I had been led before and went right up to Captain Hansen's office. He didn't stand when I entered.

"Christ, Burke, you're a mess," he observed.

"Thanks to your boys no doubt," I managed.

"I don't know what in God's name you're talking about."

As he talked the desk sergeant and another uniformed officer grabbed me by the shoulders but I twisted violently.

"Leave him be," ordered Hansen. "Get me Duffy. Tell him to come right in. Close the door for now."

The sergeant obeyed with a short nod, leaving with the other officer and closing the door.

"What happened?"

"You know what happened," I told him, indignant.

"I'm gonna go ahead and tell you that whatever did happen out there didn't have anything to do with me or any of my men. I'm also gonna remind you that I was straight with you once before, giving you the benefit of the doubt, which you obviously didn't think much of. I can see you've already got worse than you would have ever suffered on my watch so I won't dwell on it too much. But I did tell you." He allowed me to consider this.

I had come in ripped with the rye still burning hot in my gut, but with each word Hansen spoke I found it more difficult to stay motivated. My attention wavered when the old-salt cop came in and stood near me. I stood there next to him, both of us facing Hansen. Hansen addressed the cop while I looked on.

"When's the last time you saw this guy Duff?"

Duffy looked me up and down, unimpressed as ever.

"Evening before last, Cap. Followed him from here out over Deer Island. Left him at the town line. He pumped gas and bought something inside. Last I saw, he drove off. He waved."

"You strike him? You or Richardson rough him up that day or any other day? Hansen asked calmly.

"No sir. Never laid a finger on him. Neither of us."

Hansen was satisfied.

"Thanks, Duff. You can go."

Duffy left silently without giving me the time of day.

Hansen turned in his chair to open the window behind him. From his desk drawer he pulled a cigar which he prepared and lit, tossing his match out the window.

"Why don't you have a seat?" he puffed. It seemed like a good idea so I did.

"You have smokes," he asked. I nodded. "You better have one. Looks like you could have had a concussion." Hansen walked out of the office leaving the door open, the cigar in his teeth.

I finally found the smokes in my hip pocket and lit up using one of Hansen's matches which landed on the windowsill when I tossed it. Hansen returned and went around to his desk. He saw the match on the sill, picked it up, and tossed it outside.

"I'm gonna keep on being straight with you. I want you gone. But I don't get any thrills off seeing you like this," he said.

"It wasn't your guys? Fine. But you know who did, I'd wager."

"It might be that I do, but I'm telling you it don't do no good to know. What you're up under right now, you could have a hard time getting out of it."

"You got out of it. It got out of town and you said good riddance. I'd have liked to have been here for the whole investigation. That must have been some stellar work on your behalf."

"Are you screwy, Burke? I'm being friendly which I don't have to be. You think I don't have superiors? The Essex DA is right down the street. You'd like to go have a word with him too? You might be able to run things all loose in Boston. But we got a good thing going here. People still live decent and keep simple pleasures and concerns. I gotta go out there and look them in the eye every day, ask them how the children are. And the second I get the chance to assure someone that we caught the killer next door, I don't hesitate. And I take joy in the peacefulness that comes for a time being after," he said.

"I get it. You gotta look away sometimes. That makes it easy to sleep at night."

"When my kids come home from school. When my wife lies down beside me at the end of the day, that's what eases me." He said it plainly and meant it, continuing to smoke thoughtfully. "You've had your share of life. I can see it on you. But you have to stop sometimes and ponder and say, What have

I got to show for it? And what meaning does it have to me? You got anything like that, Burke? You got anything to show for all your brazen dedication?"

"I got a helluva headache."

These witty retorts were really taking it out of me. The guy's only doing what he has to. Sorry pal. So am I. I finally picked up the coffee mug and downed it in a few gulps—noticing the amount of vomit that had accumulated on my jacket sleeve. A medic came in and shined a light in my eyes, took my blood pressure, stuff like that. Hansen watched for a while, eventually turning his attention outside the window.

"You're suffering from a fairly serious concussion," the medic told me, shuffling around in a bag. He pulled out a couple of pills and had me wash them down. "I've given you a mild amphetamine. Do you know what that is?"

"Sure," I did.

"You're to take rest but not sleep for the next twenty-four hours, if possible."

"No doing," I told him. "I'm on the job."

"No you aren't." Hansen interrupted. "You're twice as done as you were when you walked in here." Hansen stood to let the medic out of the office and followed him. "That'll be all, Doc. Thank you." When he came back, the desk sergeant was with him.

"Just fine," I said without being asked.

"I'm holding you here overnight," Hansen told me. "We got an empty holding cell so you'll be comfortable, at least."

I started to stand and the whole room shifted.

"One of the boys will keep an eye on you so you don't pass out and die all over my precinct. Then you're outta here. For good."

"No thanks, Cap. I got work to do and jobs to get done."

I tried to walk past the two men, but my legs resisted, and I ended up hugging the sergeant around the shoulders as I fell forward. He was a champ and took most of my weight, dragging me to my feet and, through no help of my own, got me from Hansen's office and into a holding cell. The best digs I'd had in days. The pills the doc gave me were dissolving in the rye, commingling with the pain relievers and giving me the clarity of judgment that comes when your brain is forced through a pinhole. I sat on the wooden bench lining one of the three walls of the cell. Steel bars comprised the fourth wall before me, intersecting my vision. I spent the next several hours fidgeting. I may have dozed but for no accountable time, and if the sweet wash of sleep had passed over it was always broken by the shout of the desk sergeant.

Could it be true that Duffy really hadn't whacked me? He didn't seem too concerned when questioned. Hansen was straightforward enough, even had an air of honesty about him. If that was the case, it meant that I was deeper than I or even Hansen had considered. Unless he had considered it and believes that he really is acting in everyone's best interest by keeping something under wraps and me under lock and key.

"Hey, Sarge. How about you let me use the phone to check my messages?" I called out.

He didn't bite, kept filling out some paperwork that seemed never-ending. My legs had reestablished communication with my brain. I used them to walk about the cramped cell, swinging my arms across my chest and back, lifting them high overhead, breathing in deep. Quite a while must have gone by because the numb puffiness of the booze had dissipated, allowing my mind to come up for air, which kept happening in waves. The bullpen surrounding my cell had grown dark. The desk sergeant had gone. A night clerk stood behind the receiving desk looking at a newspaper. I craned my neck around the front of the cell trying to see down the hallway toward Hansen's office. He was walking up in my direction carrying his jacket and hat with him. When he got to the cell, he opened the door in the steel bars.

"You get your wits about you yet?" he asked.

"Don't think so."

"Time to go, anyhow. Got your vehicle parked right outside. I don't think I have to tell you but I don't expect to be seeing you again around Amesbury. You had a shot at glory but that's all over now."

Hansen walked away putting on his jacket. I took my own jacket and walked out the open cell passing by the night clerk and outside to find the Chevy parked where I felt I left it with the keys still in it.

When I got within a couple blocks of Nancy's I parked off the road under the bushes. I felt for the cold hunk of my .38 revolver, still strapped to the underneath of my seat cushion. A hiding spot I carried over from the Buick when I sold it. Even with things as rough as they were, I left the canon strapped in its spot. I grabbed a flash from the glove box and put out my smoke. I walked to Nancy's driveway and stopped, listening for any noise that may give away some hiding person. When I was certain no one was around, I headed back to the cottage around the far side of the main house, opening up on a cut-grass yard bordered by forest that wrapped all around and behind the cottage where Nancy stayed.

I tried the knob to the cottage, locked. I knocked and put my ear to the door. I shined the flash inside a window and could see Nancy wasn't home. I pressed the door and could feel a give in the old wood. I considered busting the thing down but found a window around back with a closure only strong enough to keep honest folks out. I wasn't one of those folks right now and, with my old penknife, was able to lift the latch and climb through the window. Once inside, I closed the latch and started to paw around in the dark, looking over some of the stuff in Nancy's place again. I looked in the dresser drawer for her bundle of clippings. I was still searching when I heard some crunching around outside one of the windows. I crouched. The sound of at least one person could be heard moving around the cottage. Could be Nancy, spooked, and with reason. It wasn't Nancy though.

"He was around here, Charlie, I saw it," he said to Charlie, apparently.

The beam of a flashlight came in through the windows and over my head, lighting up the far wall.

"What about the girl?" asked Charlie, "And turn that light off."

"I don't see a sign of either," said the first.

"That's his car up the street, isn't it?"

"Yeah."

"Then he's around here somewhere. Go check around the front of the main house again, and keep that light away."

The first guy retreated, his footsteps growing quieter.

Charlie stood, perhaps watching his friend, making sure he didn't get into any trouble on the way to the front house. Then I heard a slow and deliberate footstep. There was no crack of a twig as Charlie moved and if he took another step after, I couldn't tell. Near the next window, a shadow. There was a creak of pressure as Charlie pressed his hand against the window, pushing inward. The latch held, and the window stayed shut. Charlie's buddy came up to him.

"I swear he disappeared. You see anything?"

"No. Let's get out of here," said Charlie.

"We gotta go back into town? You think he gave us the slip and's looking for a place to stay?"

"He isn't staying anywhere if he's smart."

I was already slipping out the front door.

Back at the Chevy, I got in and laid down in the front putting my hand on the .38 and caught my breath.

It wasn't too long before tires started approaching on the unpaved road. Flashlight beams probing the interior of the Chevy but not giving me away. I waited like that until I couldn't hear the sound of the car on the road. I started the Chevy and followed after, keeping the headlights off and navigating only by avoiding the very darkness of the woods lining the road.

The guys drove to the town square and stopped at the main intersection. I expected one of them to get out and part ways here, calling it quits on tonight's local militia meeting, but they didn't. They didn't head further into town either. Instead, they headed south toward the bridge—a leg I was becoming all too familiar with.

I turned after them, keeping a block or more between us,

my lights still dark until we reached downtown Newburyport. The guys headed north out of downtown following the streets that intertwine in and around the port. Before long we were surrounded by loading docks of warehouses leading to the nearby water. When Charlie turned onto a short private way, I hung back and idled. I could see from where I waited that the guys drove past a guard station, partitioning off the land belonging to the Krytron Plant.

I swung the Chevy around and pulled off to the far side of a corner lot where I could still monitor the gated entrance. It was hard to believe that anyone would be committing so much of their time to haunting me to protect what was left of Donnie's reputation. Or what? Donnie had hired these guys to make sure that no one ever found him? Could be, but I'd be tough convincing. And if this guy Charlie's gonna know the real story, then why not Nancy? If Donnie had employed Charlie at all, then why would Charlie even follow through with his end of the deal? Hypothetically, Donnie's a ghost, and there's no one to hold Charlie to his end of the bargain. So what it would have to be is that Donnie's still around somewhere pulling the strings. But I still don't really buy that. It was well past midnight when the windshield had fogged over completely. It wasn't until the eastern horizon began to warm that a vehicle came up over the hill leading to the gate. When the driver got to the gate, he stopped, and the security guard popped his head out, calling the driver to come on in. Soon after that, a whole fleet of cars came up over the hill, all standing in line to pass through the gate, anxious to get the shift started so they could hurry up and have it over with. I pulled the Chevy up as close as possible without looking suspicious and idled there. Before the last of the day-shift had pulled in, another line of cars began to form.

The night-shift exited the gate to go out into the world for unsatisfying breakfast-dinners and daytime sleep that was never quite the same as rest. When finally I did see Charlie's car roll by with him alone driving, I swung out into the road, falling in line a few cars back. We drew close to the center of town, hooked down through the city center and back out toward Plum Island, returning to the bar. Charlie walked in, going all the way to the back. I could see through the open entrance that he spoke to a bartender who, after brief conversation, gave some news that upset Charlie, who walked out fast and got back into his car.

From there, we continued over onto Plum Island and into a coastal residence. Charlie parked on the street and went up to a second-floor apartment where he unlocked the door and went in.

home is the sailor

I doubled back to the narrow bar. Where the river meets the ocean could be seen out the back through a screen door. A couple of men and a woman drank at the bar, smoking. I joined them. People on the wall behind me erupted in laughter. They had pushed several tables together so they could all talk in a group.

"Drinking, mister?"

I turned to face the bartender. A tall guy with a brow that made him look like he was thinking.

"Gin with lime if you have it." He brought the gin, settling my twisted gut. I paid and tipped a five-dollar bill, which the bartender took without comment.

"Charlie stopped by earlier?" I half asked it, half told him.

The bartender didn't like it. He glanced at the barflies and over my shoulder at the pep rally.

"What was the news you had for him?"

"No news," he said. "Drink up," and started toward the back.

"I guess that means he didn't get the man he was after."

He stopped.

"I don't know what you think you're driving at but if you know Charlie then you better be on your way." This time he left and went back into the employee area.

I finished the drink and walked out the back through the screen door, listening past the back office. The bartender was on the phone, "... asking about Charlie... I told him to scram." I got back to the whip and drove over to Charlie's neighborhood again, staying a good deal away from his door when I got there. All this waiting had brought me low on the smokes but I lit up anyway, warding off sleep in the heat of the day, keeping my sight trained on that front door.

It took less than an hour for a blacked out Cadillac to roll up the block. It stopped right in front of Charlie's and idled there. The driver got out, leaving the car double-parked and walked up to Charlie's. The door opened right away, and the guy went inside. I tossed the smoke, got out of the whip, and went toward the stairs to Charlie's. A door in a fence to the side of the downstairs apartment proved to be unlocked. I slipped in. The place downstairs was quiet. The back of the building faced the seaside, which was disguised by marine layer, hanging thick despite the sun. A garbage dumpster was pushed up against the back of the apartment under a narrow terrace. I climbed up, dragging my upper half onto the deck, squirming in under the railing. I was very close to a sliding glass door covered by a curtain that was slightly cracked. Inside, Charlie and the other guy talked.

"If you didn't want to deal with the repercussions then you

shouldn't have got involved," said the stranger.

"I started out involved," said Charlie. "What do you want?"

"There was a call made. It sounds like somebody inquired about you not long after you stopped in the bar this morning."

It was quiet for a moment after that, then the stranger continued.

"Is there anybody you know that would come around and be wanting to see you?"

"No," said Charlie.

"You wouldn't think that it could be that detective come trailing after you?"

"Not likely, pal. That dick was in the weeds. Probably hiding on his belly. I left him like that when I had to."

"You should have shot him when you had the chance. Kelly painted you as a connected guy. You're acting like a washed-up old security guard."

"It wasn't the dick. He's too busy poking around back doors and getting sloshed. More likely my buddy checking up with a racing tip."

"When can we expect to have closure regarding the detective?" the stranger asked.

"I gotta work tonight, but I don't have a shift tomorrow, so sometime around then."

"It's as though you don't even want to see the situation resolved. We all have something to lose here. Perhaps it's best I advise Mr. Kelly to let your agreement lapse. Then we could hire on someone capable of completing the job and you could be disposed of in whatever way it is people like you are made to disappear."

Whatever the words meant to Charlie, they got to him. There was the crack of a fist making contact. The way I imagined it, the young stranger stumbled back after Charlie socked him.

"Take that to Kelly, you punk, for your pat on the head or wherever he's got you by. And tell him to figure out his own business if he has to. I'm taking care of myself from here on out. Starting with that lousy dick." I chanced a look inside and saw Charlie imposing over what proved to be a fairly young looking guy with a bloody welt already engulfing one eye.

"I know exactly the words I'll use to express my opinion to Mr. Kelly on the best course of action regarding your case."

"Fancy talk, no doubt. Remember whatever does happen it's you I'll be watching."

"Seems that you should be more worried about who it is whom watches you."

The stranger left it at that and backed out the front door, which Charlie slammed. The Cadillac roared away. I pulled back as he slid it shut and closed the latch. I hung and jumped down the way I came. When I heard the front door open and footsteps down the stairs, I sprinted back toward where I'd parked. Charlie was on the move, and he had me running again. I hadn't quite made it to the Chevy when he went tearing by, not noticing the familiar car on his block.

I had a good idea where he was off to, so I didn't follow too closely when he blew a stop sign not long after getting off the island.

When I pulled up across the street from the bar, I could see again inside and all the way through to the river. There were still a couple of barflies on stools, but they ignored, or were oblivious of Charlie, who was in the back and had the bartender up against the wall. They were mostly silhouettes, but it's not hard to tell when someone's getting shown what it's like, and Charlie was showing the bartender now. He left the bartender on the floor in the hall and went into the private office most likely to make a phone call.

We drove back the way we had come that morning, leaving the main town area as the residential blocks crept up. Charlie turned down one of the side streets into a neighborhood that was far less impressive than the downtown and even less so than Charlie's seaside apartment. Though the blocks were lined with two and three-story homes of historic design, they had been allowed to deteriorate. The evergreens marking the property lines had encroached, their limbs reaching out to brush against the eaves, casting shadows that cooled the wet, overgrown lawns. Woven through by chlorophyll blades: a child's plaything or a vehicle in the long-drawn-out process of repair sat abandoned.

Charlie parked in front of one of these places and got out. As he walked up the steps, I passed and went to the end of the block, banging around and parking at the intersection. The young stranger at Charlie's house was an unexpected newcomer, and part of me wished that I had acted quickly enough to have followed him instead of following Charlie. Whatever this guy Kelly had over Charlie scared him. A couple of wise guys would be real interested in finding Charlie by the sounds of it, and Kelly would have access to Charlie's personal and illegitimate history if it truly did exist. That would put the young stranger's boss in a fairly high position of authority.

The name Kelly was more than common in this area, would probably saturate the directory of Massachusetts government officials. Whatever Charlie was into right now wasn't in the playbook. If ever Charlie was liable to slip up it would be now.

"Can I get a smoke, mister?" A kid had come up beside the car without my even noticing. He was tall and gaunt. Probably always getting mistaken as older than he really was.

"What would your mother say?"

"What are you waiting over here for anyway?" he asked, and I practically threw the stick at him to halt the line of questioning.

"Do you know who lives in that house?" I pointed near Charlie's car.

"Of course I do," said the kid, "I know everyone on this street."

"So who is it?"

"Mister, I don't believe that's any of your business."

The kid adopted a steely face and looked me over. His face changed when I slid a fiver out of my stash, holding it folded in between my fingers.

"I work for the bank. The man that lives in that house owes money to the bank for a mortgage. You know what a mortgage is?"

"Sure."

He looked down his cigarette at me.

"Then you know that if you don't pay a mortgage you could lose the house. It's my job to follow up on people like this. All I need to know is if the man who pulled up is the man who always lives there." The kid didn't believe me, and he didn't have to as long as he was glancing at the fiver the way he was.

"The man that lives there is named Dale Pinkard. He's lived

there for a long time. Works right down the street at that Krytron Plant. That wasn't him that pulled up."

I pretended to contemplate this information while the kid grew increasingly anxious.

"Just fine," I said after a long moment.

I handed the kid the bill and he snatched it, tossing his smoke on the ground. I watched him go in my rearview until he rounded a corner and disappeared into the neighborhood. Dale must be the guy Charlie was nosing around with the other night. Charlie had mentioned that he worked this evening so he came here no doubt in order to task Dale with the burden of finding me. Lucky for him I was planning on making it an easy job. When Charlie left, I let him go. It was getting dark when the garage attached to Dale's place opened up and he pulled out in a car that was in near-perfect condition, as though Dale only drove to work, or out of necessity, and not in the winter at all by the look of the paint and trim around the bottom of the chassis. He drove like I was right, which made the trip back to Amesbury tedious. It was my impression that once crossing over the bridge and Deer Island, as Duffy had named it, we would progress to the north side of town to scope out Nancy's place for any sign of me or her. Dale did not go this way, and we stayed on the south side in a commercial district which began as diners and shops and led to liquor stores and what looked like a gentleman's club on one block. Dale stopped in front of a general store and got out. But instead of going into the store, he went around the side and up a set of wooden steps leading to an apartment above. I waited for the door to close behind him, then parked up the block and walked back, keeping an eye on the top of the staircase. I got to the storefront and lingered for a second before turning the corner. At the bottom of the steps were a few mailboxes drilled to the wall for when they split a place like this into several separate units. They were marked up crudely with tape or metal placards and when I shined the flash for a brief moment, one stood out: Brighton #2B

I walked over the nails that had been driven into the steps, avoiding the creaky center. I stopped to listen in the apartment above. Everything was silent. There were two doors on the landing: 2A and 2B. Another set of stairs broke off from here and continued up to a third floor. I pressed my ear to 2B and felt the handle. It was silent.

The handle turned.

I opened the door a crack, and now could hear the sounds of laughter coming from somewhere inside the place. I couldn't make out any of the lines, but every few seconds, the airy roars exploded on cue with clapping and whistling. I closed the door, trapping the game show noise inside with me.

The entryway of Donnie's apartment was a kitchen and living room all in one with the carpet stopping halfway between. It was quickly apparent that Donnie had not taken much time to decorate the place, or had taken the time to clean up very well before taking off. There were no photos around, no paperwork or mail near the table at the door. No handwritten notes on the icebox, not even a magazine near the sofa. I half-heartedly searched the sofa cushions.

Dale chuckled in the next room.

The broadcast had lulled me into forgetting I wasn't alone.

The next room was a bedroom. Bare walls with a bed, chair, and television. Dale sat in the wooden chair down near the end of the bed facing the television with his arms crossed over his chest. He turned his head real slow, shoulders never shifting. His face silhouetted by the glowing tube in the curtained room.

"Hey there, Dale," I said.

He lunged from where he was, knocking the chair back into the wall. Up until now I had considered Dale to be the dull type, but when he got the best of me, it hurt and made me reconsider what it was to pass judgment. His fist heated the air as he swung at my face which I accepted without ever moving from the door jamb. I got my hands up for the next, deflecting several well-timed jabs from the sly ox who danced around so much I was half-expecting to see a girl come out with a sign at the bell. When I swung, he dodged, keeping his fists at his sides, waiting for me to overstep, which I did. His body shot up from the knees and his fist from his hip, catching me right under the chin, knocking my teeth into my brain. The wall caught me. I spit the blood from my mouth. Dale closed in. This time his fist clutched a canon. I dove at Dale and the gun went off, putting a hole in the wall. I hit him low with my shoulder, digging into his belly, doubling him over, and heaving upward on the great weight of the man before dropping him to the floor, driving my whole body into his abdomen. There was a crack and Dale sputtered, releasing the gun from his hand. I grabbed it, and crouched over him.

"Where's Donnie Brighton?" I asked him.

"Shove off." He struggled to speak.

"You've certainly put us both through a lot for shove off."

"Why don't you let things alone? No one needs to know." Dale continued to clutch at his side, hopefully nothing too important was broken.

"If that was true I wouldn't be here. Donnie has his reasons for hiding, I get it. But I don't get what's the worth in helping him hide.

"There's a reason for each," he said.

"Think of the kid's mother."

"Think of mine."

"How'd you and Charlie make me to begin with?

"Go back to Boston. Let us alone."

His body convulsed, and I would have thought seizure if not for the thump of the compressed pistol rounds that were buried in Dale's chest. I turned to see a man in the doorway, covered up in a full-length trench coat. He wore a brimmed hat, formal shoes, and patterned socks with slacks. He pointed a pistol in my direction. It was a special automatic job with a custom hammer and pearlescent grip. Putting my back to the wall, I leveled Dale's gun but not level enough. The doorframe erupted in woodchips. The figure disappeared out and down the stairs. I got to the door only in time to see a forgettable sedan peeling away.

I returned to Dale's body and knelt over him, but he was dead. I wiped his gun and put it near his body. The canned laughter resumed in the next room. From this angle, I noticed under the bed, illuminated by the television: a metallic canister, a film canister. Judging by the weight of it, film would still be inside. I pocketed the canister, scanning the room for any other trace of my being there. Even in this part of town, a gunshot wouldn't be outright ignored, and the police would arrive eventually. The right thing to do, I thought as I climbed into the heap, was to wait for responding officers or contact Hansen outright. He should be informed that there was a murder and that Charlie and Dale are up to something that has to do with Donnie. The film canister should be surrendered right away to evidence for development by a forensics officer or, in a town like this, the coroner. The last thing I would want to do is fail to report a homicide which, if I did, could result in the loss of my license, and likely what dwindling reputation I had left.

Returning to Main Street, I headed for the north side of town. I kept my head down as a couple of cruisers sped by in the opposite direction, going to Arthur's to investigate. Most of the thoughts I had of Donnie's being a simple man on the run had vanished when Dale was killed. When the sun was down, I clicked the high beams on. The next sign I saw was urging me to drive with courtesy, insisting it to be 'The New Hampshire way.' The sign after that was for a place called Exeter.

"I can't promise they'll all come out but I can try for you," the pharmacist said, handling the canister.

"Please. Anything you could get would be appreciated. My dear mother's sister has passed unexpectedly.

"My condolences," he offered, writing up a ticket for the film. "Was she a woman of the town? I likely knew her."

"I'm passing through on my way to Vermont where she lived."

"Usually these things take time." He apologized with his expression.

"I was hoping there could be a special exception made. The

service is tomorrow. Whatever it takes."

I presented four times the amount the developed roll would actually cost, and the man's face changed. What was such an endearing look was now tinged with desire as he eyed the bills and weighed the business he would lose against gaining mine. The math worked in my favor, and he finished writing the ticket. He took the money sheepishly and put it under the till.

"I hate to ask for anything really... but a man has to eat."

"You're doing me a favor and I thank you." Between my personality and my bankroll, everyone was on my side. "May I come back in the morning?"

"I'm up and open every day at six on the dot."

"I'll hold you to it."

I lit up when I got outside. I needed to eat. I needed some sleep. I put the ticket for the film in the glove box. I got the rye out and took a long pull. I started up the Chevy and headed south.

I knocked, and Nancy let me in. A phonograph played in the corner. The bare bulb cast an orange hue. The stove was warm, "Coffee?"

I slugged down a cup of coffee, and had my fill of fresh water, and cheese sandwiches with some roast beef and mustard. I must have made quite a scene because, when I did look up for once, she was sitting across from me looking on, in shock.

"Thanks for the grub, kid. Solid."

"You obviously needed it. Should I ask if there's any news about Donnie?"

"It's been tough going to be honest. Where have you been?"

"I was in Haverhill checking in on mother. I go there to see her at least once a week. I don't feel right leaving her alone so much, but also I get the feeling that I should be close to here in case Donnie comes back. I know it sounds foolish, but that's how I feel."

"Nothing's foolish when you feel it," I told her. "Before you took off for your ma's did you notice anything strange? You sense anything or see something suspicious?"

"I'm not sure what you mean. I get a lot of looks when I go into town. Not so much now that it's been some time."

"What about around here? Anyone snooping around?"

"Besides you?"

"What about following you?"

"Would I know if I were being followed?"

"Depends. Sometimes you get a sense or, start seeing a new person more often."

"I'm afraid I haven't been thinking very clearly lately."

"Listen. I can't tell you what to do but I don't like the idea of your staying around here alone."

Her eyes shifted and she was flushed.

"Relax. It's not a proposition."

"Of course not. It's only that I would much rather be here in town."

"What about your mother's?"

"I could go there, but I would only worry. She would know that something was wrong. I appreciate your advice, I do. But I have to be here for my brother."

"That's fine. I can't force you. But you should know that there have been a couple of hired guys hanging around here.

I ran into them the other night and last. The first time we met didn't go so well for me. The other not so well for one of them."

"I should have been here. I could have helped you."

"These guys aren't screwing around. With what's happened today they're gonna be anything but reasonable. You gotta stay here. I get it. But you should be warned, you're in danger."

"Danger? Then something terrible has happened to Donnie. I knew it."

The sobbing started from out of nowhere, as if there were a switch, and then stopped. She pulled herself together, and I handed her a fresh smoke.

"I'll stay, and that's final. I'm not going to be bullied around by the media and the police and now every faceless man knocking on my door. Let them come. I'll be right here waiting." She was adamant.

"Like I said, I can't force you."

Hopefully her stones withheld if Charlie came dropping in. Hopefully that was something we didn't have to worry about.

"How well did you know anyone down at the Krytron Plant?

"Not very well at all. The only person I ever heard him talk about was Cliff and that was after everything."

"What about Charlie? Or Dale Pinkard? Those names mean anything to you?"

"I'm sure I don't know."

"What about the name Kelly?"

"I wish I could be of more help but I've had limited contact with Donnie up until all of this. Outside of what's in his letters, I don't know much about him."

"I know it might be hard right now, but could you read

through some of those letters for me, Nance? Try to look at them differently and see whether there's anything else that stands out."

"I'll try."

The phonograph stopped.

Nancy started, about to get up.

"I'll get it."

I took the empty sandwich plate and my cup to the sink and cleared the dishes. I flipped the record to the B-side and lowered the needle from its position. The album continued, something old. I recognized the tune, but didn't know the words. Again, I found myself looking at the photos on the wall, inspecting the expressions on all of the faces, made blurry by the graininess of the image. I looked again at the smiles of the men on the submarine deck. The pistols they each wore were of Naval issue, commemorative jobs probably handed out in a ceremony. Each had been customized, featuring a special grip and hammer. Each matched the weapon used to kill Dale earlier that night.

"Do you know anyone in these photos?"

"Who?" Nancy asked.

"These men, do you know them?"

"No. They must be people from town."

I took the photo off the wall and brought it to the table.

I unclipped the latches from the back and popped out the cardboard insert. The back of the photo was blank white except for some faint pencil markings:

Tirante SS-420 '44

I took the photo.

"I have to go."

"Now?"

"Think about what I said."

"You know I'm not going anywhere, Mr. Burke."

"You have my card. Call my service if you decide to leave or if anything happens. I'll check in as soon as I can."

"Can't you tell me where you're going?"

"It's starting to look like the less involved you are the better."

I got in the whip and drove off, speeding.

Nancy was a hard nut and I like that. Some of the best guys I know were real hard nuts before they got cracked. I passed again the sign welcoming me to New Hampshire. Whoever shot Dale had done it with a Navy-issue service automatic. Like the two in the old photo at Nancy's. The Naval Yard in Portsmouth was famed for turning out submarines like sandwiches and, in its heyday, launched up to four vessels daily, many of which would be earning confirmed ships sank in the Pacific and other foreign depths. It was almost ten years ago that all of the wartime prisoners held in the Naval Prison had been released. It was rumored that when engineers inspected the German U-boats, those prisoners had been captured in, they were found to contain a plethora of odds and ends like developmental plans for conceptual weapons and a hefty payload of uranium oxide. The Yard was still running at full capacity, as it had since being federalized at the start of the nineteenth century. The guys who work there now are ex-servicemen. Those ex-servicemen could have served on the Tirante. Some of them may even have a custom-job automatic with a pearl grip. It was a flimsy lead to build any suspicion on but, at this point, flimsy would do.

a man about a boat

Before I knew it, I had cut clear across the bottom of New Hampshire and was inside Maine. I followed the smell of salt and soon was driving along a familiar scene, which was all coastal towns.

The village up the hill and behind me was punctuated by a single street before reaching the boundary of the dock yard. This was not an area under Navy jurisdiction, but it was certainly their territory. From here, the island constituting the Naval Yard and prison could be seen clearly, and their presence hung in the air. The ships that docked near mainland were of all makes, hauling containers, or tourists headed up to Nova Scotia, pontoons, and trolling boats were lined up at wooden docks and even anchored in rows wherever space would allow. Across the main drag, buildings stood in a similar fashion, crammed in a row where space would allow, offering refuge for sailors and some cheap thrills for whoever wanted them. I made my way down the block casually, not quite knowing what I was looking for. I passed by a dingy bait shop and general store that had no signs, but stacked its wares in front windows. After that was a couple of converted homes turned into offices, salvage, insurance, import, export. There were different signs over each ground-level door and then another by the steps that led to the upstairs of each. Judging by the look of the signs, the separate businesses had a singular owner. I considered stepping inside to ask around for Mack but didn't like the idea of showing my face to the record-keeping, wax-stamping, face-remembering guy that would work inside. The flop house next door drew my attention instead.

Dilapidated shutters hung onto rotting siding. The front rose up in spires, pocked with warped glass windows that marked the rooms inside. The shingled peaks were formed at varying levels due to design, or happenstance. I crossed the street, avoiding the sparse traffic, and walked up the front steps. I checked around. There was no one nearby that seemed to care whether I came or went, so I ducked inside. The inside of the place was what I'd expect from looking at the exterior. The anteroom and coat wall past the inside of the door had been turned into a lobby you'd see at a bed-and-breakfast. There were no elderly couples or bridge clubs set up in the sitting room, though. The windows had been darkened to keep out the sunlight. The high-backed armchairs surrounding a burnt-out fireplace had become tattered with age and indiscriminate use. What was a dining area, branching off from the opposite side of the lobby had been turned into an office. A heavy drape, which acted as the doorway between the office and the hall where I stood, was tied partially back with a piece of rope. A clerk's desk had been built in front of that. The desktop was empty and the post unmanned. A fireplace with a cooking rack burned on the far wall in the office, casting shadows of the books and junk that had been piled up on the old dining table. I knocked on the top of the desk and got no response. I listened, heard nothing, waited quietly for a minute, and then crept around the desk to peek into the office. As I grasped the curtain to pull it back, I found myself with my nose in the chest of a hulking man who looked down at me from on high, which was probably a good foot above the top of my head. I could fit two of my feet in each of his shoes which were draped over by his unhemmed slacks. He appraised me, toes to nose in one glance. And then, adjusting what I realized was a knitted afghan wrapped around his shoulders, he turned away.

"No rooms," he said plainly, going back to the office.

I pulled out my bankroll and the sound of the bills stopped him.

"What does it cost to room here, anyway?"

He turned back around, and this time I could have swore he grew another foot.

"Have you got corn in your ears, pal? I said beat it."

His voice faltered, and he went into a coughing fit.

"All right, take it easy. I'm not looking for any problems."

He wanted to talk again, but the coughing had taken hold of him, gripping his chest and was pulling him toward the ground. His face swelled and turned red. I put the cash away and grabbed him by the arm. He batted me away but didn't try very hard, and I got my shoulder under him enough to get him to a chair, not dragging him by any means but more like leading him as one leads a horse.

"You better get out of here, pal," he managed in between wheezes.

"The tough guy act isn't working, so drop it. You have an asthma device or something? A prescription?"

"Nah."

"Allergies?"

"Nuh, uh."

"Anxiety?"

"Listen here."

He was overcome by another fit of coughing. Having been polite for about as long as I could, I took a handkerchief out and used it to cover my mouth and nose while the big guy went on expectorating. It was some time before he stopped.

"I got a cold."

"Sure it's not a pneumonia?"

"I think I've had about enough of you."

"I didn't mean anything by it."

"Give me a smoke."

I did, against my better judgment and, when he held it in his teeth, I lit it up for him. His hand shook as he handled the smoke, but he didn't cough again and immediately became more relaxed.

The guy took a long drag. He looked at me through the rising smoke, I could see that his eyes glistened. I patted him on the knee as I rose.

"I know what would fix you. I'll be right back."

"Get the hell out of here, you crazy bastard!"

But he didn't quite finish. The coughing took him over as

I stepped outside.

It didn't take long for me to get what I needed, a half pint of whiskey from a liquor store down the block. Further on, I found a grocer's market with some lemons growing in terra-cotta pots outside. I grabbed a few. I dug my nail in, and the citrus escaped. They would have fought hard to grow here at this time of year. I went in holding them in my hands. An elderly lady was in the process of packing up her coin purse when I arrived, and I waited patiently for her to finish. She handled the pieces as if they were about to stop minting them, and I'm sure she knew the amount in the purse at all times, adjusting the total in her head as she spent or received each penny. She'd never have time to spend it all at the rate she was going. The thought of Donnie crossed my mind, tinted a healthy brown by the rich rays of the sun riding low on the equator, where warm crystal waters lapped white sandy beaches. He looked at me through darkened sunglasses, and could I make out the glint of his eye? Or was it some illusion created by the gleam of paradise reflected in the lenses. The lady began the next leg of her trek, shuffling toward the exit door.

"Fresh lemons, mister. Grown them myself," said the man behind the counter. The wrinkles on his face were plenty, but the skin was smooth in between.

"That's swell," I said.

"Anything else?"

"A cinnamon stick and honey and some nutmeg if you have it."

"Ah," said the old man, "I see what you're after."

He moved from behind the counter and walked about the store, taking things from shelves as he went.

"Been spending a couple of nights down at Cathy's, have you? Most don't have the sense to take care of themselves coming out of there. They think a quick scrubbing, and changing their britches is enough." He winked at me, knowingly.

He returned carrying a handful of items and laid them out next to the lemons on the counter.

"I don't have the nutmeg, but here's some ginger. That'll give you a zing. And if you spent your time right, you need rest more than anything," with another lecherous wink, "so here's a bundle of dried chamomile. A couple pinches will get you through the night. Hope you wake up in time to ship out!"

Back out on the street, I tightened my collar with one hand, jostling the bag around in one arm until finally situating the package in the crook of my arm. At the far end of the block was some shouting and commotion, a group of derelicts arguing over the ownership of some indiscernible object. I got back inside the flophouse without knocking and went right past the lobby into the dining room office. The clerk hadn't moved from the chair where I left him before. I pushed some papers aside from the dining room table and laid out the groceries. The clerk watched me as I did.

"Why don't you leave me alone? Don't make me get mean."

"You got a kitchen?" I asked.

The clerk nodded in the direction of the lobby. I went out that way and past the staircase, down the hall, where I found myself in a kitchen left over from when the place was a home. The open door had a sign that designated the kitchen as "private." I found a kettle that would withstand the fireplace and filled it with water from the tap of a sink that could have passed for a mop bucket, though the water that ran out untainted.

I found a couple of mugs that looked safe enough to drink from and rinsed them out. I took these things with me and closed the door behind. On the wall of the staircase, below where the banister met the second floor, hung a directory with a slim mail slot for each resident. The names on each room were written with chalk and they were all occupied, as the clerk had said. I didn't notice any worthwhile names, but the top unit was marked, *MANAGER* and under that a name, *PASTOR*.

I placed the kettle on the cooking rack in the fireplace and took a bit of the cinnamon, ginger, and chamomile, adding it to the steaming water while the clerk continued to eye me like a cornered animal.

"How long you been feeling like this?"

"What are you, a doctor?"

I poured the whiskey into the mugs and brought one over to him. He took it, hand shaking again, and pressed the mug to his lips. We drank. The fire heated the kettle.

"You, Pastor?"

"Nah, Hank Trevisani," he spoke thickly.

"Out on the directory it says Pastor."

Hank liked this.

"That's from my old man. He was a priest in the old country but, around here, everyone called him pastor. I don't think he cared for it very much, but it stuck."

"How'd he get into the landlord business?"

"He didn't really mean to, I figure. See, there's no church anywhere before you get up the hill into town. Pop, he wanted to be of service to the guys who didn't have time to get into town or couldn't risk showing their faces too far off the dock. So he bought this place."

"Kind of like a docking sanctuary?"

"Yeah, I guess. Half of every ship that landed would go down the block to Cathy's, and the other half would come here then before long the other half would pass through looking to pay penance before shipping out again."

"He must have made a living for himself."

"He was too high and mighty to be taking any payment, said it was sacrilege. This is a historic building you're in. Been around since they started modernizing the Naval Yard. Some Navy hot shot named Ford owns all the buildings like that around here. You've heard of him."

I hadn't.

"Well, Ford owns a bunch of places like this, even owns Cathy's, it's also a historic building. Pop always got a real good deal on rent, and the town liked having an upstanding preacher in their midst, so mostly he got along spreading the good word in here free of charge. It was me that convinced him to start renting rooms for profit, under the table. He didn't like that either, but even the holy have to eat, so I came back here and started running the rooms for him, on the QT, of course. I keep his title on the directory out there 'cause I think the guys like to remember when he was here. I do, too."

As we drank, he became looser and more human.

He was practically jovial.

"Hey, how about another smoke?"

I gave him one and lit my own.

"I'm gonna end up owing you."

I waved him off. "You could give me some advice though."

"You mean information? I used to be a hotel dick in Manhattan before coming home to help pop. Where do you think I got the idea to rent rooms? I know the score. A guy in your position, being friendly, always has a bottom line."

"I should've tried to get you drunk instead of well."

"It wouldn't have done you any better. Besides, I got nothing to hide, and you've been friendly in a real way."

"The names Burke. You can call me Joe, if you like."

I handed him a card.

"You with the bank?"

"I'm looking for a boat."

"What has he done now, the crazy bastard?"

"Who?"

"He used to be one of pop's most faithful customers. If there was ever a person that needed absolving, it was Mack. You from the courthouse, or what?"

"Not at all."

"Mack done anything too bad?"

"Nothing. I want to talk to him."

"You looking for clams?"

He let out a laugh that came out like a cough. I got up, took his mug, and went to the kettle. I cut open a lemon with my pocket knife and squeezed the juice from one half into Hank's mug. I scraped out some honey and let that drip into the mug. The kettle was hot. I poured the water using the knife to stir the contents of the mug, melting the honey. I used the whiskey to fill the rest of the cup and brought it back over to Hank. He breathed deeply as spices commingled with the chamomile. He drank and I could practically feel the effects of the elixir myself. I poured another slug of whiskey into my own glass and sipped it.

"When pop died, I took the place over. Guys would still come through looking for their absolution, and I'd wring them for the price of the room instead. A fella's gotta have a place to sleep, clean conscious or not, and I wasn't afraid to capitalize on it. Pop probably wouldn't have liked it."

"You think I could find Mack down at Cathy's with a girl?"

"Mack? Not very likely. He can barely get his feet under him most times, never mind anything else. Besides, Cathy's girls are for out-of-towners. Some of the local boys still go in every now and again but only those who have a special relationship."

"You ever been?"

"Not since I come back from the city. I seen a lot of things in that city. Didn't feel so right bothering those girls after that. You could have yourself some fun down there though, if you're asking."

"I'm not. I want to know where to find a boat."

"Real professional. I could have learned a few plays from you back in the day."

"So, if not at Cathy's, then where do you think I would find Mack?"

Hank yawned, opening a gaping mouth. He smacked his lips. "Mack's a drunk."

"Ah," I said.

"There's only one place you need to look to find a drunk."

"And where might that be around here?"

"At Cathy's," said Hank smiling to himself, finishing the tea, the effects of which may have been working too good.

"Hank? Come on, pal. You pulling my leg now? You said those girls weren't for locals."

"You know the job description of the hotel dick?" he asked. I got the feeling he was going to tell me. "Toss working dames, toss drunks, break up card games. Funny, I come back here to get away from it all, and here you come, and what do you want to know about? Dames and drunks and card games."

"Some things you can't get away from, but I really gotta know where to find Mack."

"Nah, tell them Hank sent you." He kept the mug held in his hands, chest heaving evenly. He was asleep.

I left the flophouse silently, leaving Hank to his peace. I laid a couple of smokes for him on a table next to his giant elbow, a couple more nails. The son of a preacher, a hotel snoop, an immigrant, a flophouse proprietor. He said he didn't go to Cathy's anymore. Maybe the girls don't ask him around there any more. Brothels are a strange thing. In most cases, everyone in a town is aware the brothel is what it is and does what it does. If you were to ask an average citizen they'd flush, darting their eyes, as they explained about things of which they'd of course have no idea. This end of the block was different from the rest. A few brick apartment and office buildings had been constructed here, blocking the view of the ocean and Naval Yard from the level of the street. An alley opened on my right.

Several dwellings had been built here from whatever could be found. I saw no sign of a fight, but this was the spot where the men had been arguing earlier. Across the street and slightly up the block was a familiar-looking home built in the same fashion as Hank's. The yard was well kept and hedged by lilac. The siding was old but painted, and the windows were curtained by new, velvety-looking draperies.

When I rang the bell, a chiming response came from inside the house. The door opened on well-oiled hinges. The carpet at my feet was purple. The lady standing in front of me held the door in one gloved hand. A cigarette burned in a holder in her free hand. She was made up with blush and eye shadow, her hair up with lace and feather. Her costume pressed her chest up so that she was all but exposed, outlined by more lace struggling to contain her. A longish petticoat covered her up some but wasn't making any great revelations in the craft. I looked her in the eyes, which were all business despite the extravagant appearance. She was older than me, younger than most, but the age was on her in the secret places and in her air. Her mouth smiled, and she showed her teeth. When she spoke, her manner was seductive though her tone had to it the definition of a person who is conducting a business they know and love and who is in charge. I'd hate to be on the wrong end of this one.

"Howdy, sailor," she said.

"You Cathy?"

"That I am. Which means, you've made it."

With that, she ushered me in and closed the door.

"It looks like you've come a long way to get here, friend."

"Hell and high water."

"You're no sailor, though. Your legs are too straight."

"I'm no sailor, only a passer-through."

"Isn't that lovely. Passing-through people are some of my favorite people. You won't get sore at me if I ask how you heard of us?"

"Not at all. I got a friend down the street. Hank."

"And how is he? It was a real shame for all of us when his daddy passed."

"The pastor?"

"Don't worry, I'm not exposing him for nothing. He was a good and honest preacher but not high and mighty like most. He'd sit in the parlor on occasion, nursing a brandy and watching the men play cards."

She took her smoke, which had extinguished as we spoke, out of the holder. She went to a crescent moon reception desk, which probably weighed more than a car and was carved with flourishes and deep lines. Padded velvet wrapped around the front, fastened with gold rivets. The velvet was purple, same as the carpet, same as the curtains. Baroque molding, ornate and protruding, joined lively red and gold cloth wallpaper to the ceiling, which supported several chandeliers hanging over a table accented by fresh-cut flowers. Cathy had replaced her smoke and offered me the same from an engraved silver case. As I lit up using Cathy's lighter, a door opened near the back of the waiting room. A girl of about twenty-five, blonde, emerged and stood, resting her hand on one of the chairs in the waiting room. Her nails were done with white tips. She stuck a hip out, and her whole body went with it. I could see the outline of her breasts beneath a sheer camisole that hung down to her thighs and, if my overactive imagination was correct, it was all she had on.

"How do you do, sir?"

"Just fine," I managed.

Cathy seemed pleased, smiling as she smoked.

"You said you know Hank from back in New York?"

"I didn't say. But yeah, I do."

"Are you a professional man like he was? Is there some case of great importance from which you can't be distracted for one moment bearing down on you?"

"Not at all."

"Then why don't you relax, Mr..."

"Burke."

"Let's get you cleaned up and fixed up, and then we'll get you a drink made up. Elsie, why don't you show Mr. Burke to a room and get him a razor."

"Yes, Miss Cathy." Elsie walked over, extending a hand, which I took.

"This really isn't necessary."

"Isn't it though?"

And I couldn't argue with her as I followed Elsie's bare legs upstairs to her room.

I shaved in the washroom without making much conversation. I could see her through the mirror by the bed lighting some candles.

"You from around here?"

"No, I'm not."

"Where from then?"

"Louisiana. It's in the south. Ever been?"

She was crawling onto the bed now.

"Yeah, I have. What brought you all the way up here?"

"All kinds of stuff," was what she said, rolling onto her back.

I rinsed my face off and looked at Elsie again in the mirror. The camisole had come off, and she was stretched out across the bed, looking at me in the reflection. I turned the light out and went to join her.

I smoked in Elsie's bed, admiring her still unclothed form as she fixed her hair in the bathroom mirror. Soon she had dressed, covering up much more than before, and left me to get myself together.

"I'll be in the second floor parlor if you want that drink, Mr. Burke."

"Sure thing."

I washed up and dressed slowly. It's a good thing Nancy hadn't floated me a fat retainer, I might have moved in here and forgot all about her. I made my way back the way I came. Elsie's room was on the third floor with the eaves. The second floor resumed the grand design of the lobby. I meandered toward the noises of music, poking my nose into the hallway doors as I went. Most of the rooms on this level weren't as nice as Elsie's. She must have been a star player, first-time customer special. When the hallway opened up, I found myself in a two-story saloon. Up where I was, it was more of a balcony that wrapped around the entire room and allowed me to look down onto the parlor below. There was a bar downstairs with a bartender done up in a fashion similar to Miss Cathy's. There was a piano and a phonograph and several tables. It was empty down there except for a table of four men playing a hand of cards. There was a bar up on this level as well, so I sat, and the bartender—a stone-faced guy with sunken cheeks and a bad haircut wearing a suit and a bow tie—served me a brandy without asking, and slid me a handwritten bill for the drink and then some. He took the bill and cash from me and deposited it into an envelope. I sat there, drinking quietly, while he cleaned some glasses. The card players talked loudly below.

"Listen to your wife, and listen to me. It's coming from the northeast, it's gonna rage for days, the likes of which you've never seen," said a man with a gruff voice.

"You say that every time the clouds change," said another, more youthful voice. "I don't know if you're trying to scare us off your haul or give yourself the excuse to stay in all weekend."

"Go out there all the seasons I have, and you'll use a scratched knuckle as an excuse to stay home."

"Must be nice. I use every excuse I can to get out of the house. I'd rather be lying ahull in fifty footers, she's been so attached lately," said the young man.

"Jus' cause that young wife of yours is too pretty and cooks too much? Is that why you can't stand her?" asked a third. "Why, if I wasn't right here I'd be over at your house giving your pretty wife what for and eating hash 'til my gut bust."

"You'll get a bust gut soon enough with a mouth like that," said the young one.

"Oh, so you do love her!" cried the third, and laughter broke out at the young man's expense. "So then I figure you will be at home all the weekend, and not out braving the swell."

Among the laughter, a fourth voice broke in: hardened and

aged, diluted by unabated drinking.

"I'd throw each one of you overboard for insubordination with talk like that. I'll be out there, fifty-foot swell or not. And I'll pay the price and a half for every pound any man can haul in more than me this weekend."

"I bet, old man," said the gruff voice. "Mack's drunk his way through so many storms he could pull a haul blind."

"He has," said the third.

"He'd tie one hand to the helm and the other to a bottle, and he'd make a better catch than you or I had all year," said the gruff man.

"And all your wives too," muttered Mack.

The men all laughed and began calling their hands again. Hank was right. Mack had a boat and, by the sounds of it, he wasn't scared to use it. A bell rang behind the bar I was at, and the bartender picked up a phone.

"Yes, ma'am," he said and then hung up.

He left me there at the bar and walked around all the way to the far end of the balcony to a door with a gold plaque affixed. Without knocking, he went in and then returned several moments later, going down the stairs, eyeing me the whole time, like he was saying, I'm leaving you here alone, but I'll know what you're doing. Nurts to you, Lurch. I raised my glass in his direction. I poured myself a second brandy, leaving the cost in cash next to the bottle. The conversation continued downstairs among the card players, and I waited to hear for when would be the best time to approach the obviously drunken Mack. I was wondering whether all of his bawdy talk could be backed up by any bravery in what sounded like a very rough, Nor'easter that was brewing off the coast.

I looked at myself in the mirror of the bar and was pleased to see that the shave had held up, no nicks or cuts to speak of. I raised my glass to myself this time and drank, looking over the assorted bottles and prizes that are acquired by any bar: a liquor license, a bent horseshoe puzzle that hadn't been undone. Some various photos had been tacked up, among them, one of a woman in her twenties. She was dressed fairly simply, though still looked very seductive, and in her expression it was easy to find that of Cathy. She must have been fifteen years younger in the picture, perhaps only working here at the time, though she had already developed those characteristics of a shrewd business person. There were photos of other girls mixed in with some stills of wild nights that had been had here over the years. When I saw the next framed image, I checked around to be sure I was still alone and crept behind the bar.

The image was that of two men, one a commander, the other a man of rank. They stood side by side near the bow of an aircraft carrier. I took the frame off the wall and laid it on the bar. I undid the clasps and removed the picture from the frame and found pencil markings on the back, similar to the photo I carried:

Tirante SS-420 1944
Homeward bound Sailor.
We gave them hell over there now give them hell over here
I'll be stationed in Kittery indefinitely
Don't fall in love with the dry land
- Sgt. Major Martin MacRury

71

I took the photo from the frame, folding it up and pocketing it. I took the duplicate from Nancy's place, smoothed it on the bar to get out some of the creases, and replaced it in the frame. As I hung the whole thing back up, what could only be the sound of a fist-making contact with bone came from downstairs.

I never found out what started the brawl. Either cheating at cards or ideas about somebody's wife would be the easy guess. When I got to the base of the steps, Lurch was already presiding over the whole fight with a baseball bat that he must have kept stashed for times like this. The thing was wrapped, and he choked it down real low, ready to swing. The four cards players were hardly concerned with the bartender and continued to throw each other around. The youngest of them was knocked back over a table and broke it in two. Lurch dragged him to his feet, the kid swung, catching the bartender in the jaw. The bat came down on the kid's arm and he let out a holler that turned him red and turned him around. He pummeled Lurch with both hands. After several feet of poor defense, Lurch dropped the bat and was in the center of the fray, which I still skirted.

A working girl opened a door at the far end of the saloon and screamed when she saw the ruckus. The door closed and one of the card players, a broad man with beard and mustache and hands like anchors grabbed at Lurch who had got the better of the young man and was wringing his neck. The bearded man took the bat off the floor and swung for the fences, getting Lurch behind the knee. Lurch crumpled, and the bearded man raised the bat again.

"Easy, Mack!" called the third, and he grabbed the bat away from Mack.

Mack turned on his three friends, who all began to restrain him. Mack was furious drunk. I made a dive at him and grabbed him around his shoulders to move him toward the door, the others reaching over me to accost their friend. I pushed the young one back, opening myself up, and got popped right in the chin by the third. I held Mack back with one arm, pushing him toward the door and, when the third swung again, I wrapped him up at the elbow with my free hand. I let go of Mack with my other and pulled the third into my oncoming fist. Something, the bat probably, caught me in the side, taking the wind out of me. Without looking, I spun and decked the guy who had hit me. It was Lurch, and I laid him out flat.

I bent to get Mack up, under his arms, straining to manage his weight. The others came pawing at both me and Mack trying to break us apart, confused whether they should help their friend or continue to beat him. We moved toward the exit as a mob, fighting the whole way until Cathy appeared at the opposite end of the saloon holding a cocked revolver with two hands, arms out, elbows bent, feet square. I pushed Mack backward out the door, and we ran through the parlor out past the front desk. I heard the sound of a gunshot and the snap of cracked wood. I looked back as we ran and saw Mack's buddies, scampering down the front stairs, all going their separate ways. Cathy, surrounded by some of her girls, stood on the porch still brandishing the pistol. I followed Mack now, who seemed to have his wits back, and moved with purpose. He crossed the street, leading me to the shanty alley I had seen on my way in. He walked all the way to the back and right up to a surprisingly impressive structure built of wood, with corrugated metal roofing and sealed with plaster.

Compared to the other shacks, Mack's was a palace with an interior the size of a city apartment. He had furnished the place with a narrow bed and even an easy chair. The decorations on the walls told of a life at sea and ports of foreign lands. Mack went inside and began to immediately search for something in the sheets and in the chair and under anything. He threw everything that wasn't what he wanted across the room. He muttered to himself, shouting now and again. When the search was apparently over but unsuccessful, he stormed out the front entrance and addressed the unseen residents of the alley.

"You miserable cowards have done it again! Robbing the only honest man among 'ya! Robbing old Mack, who got you home while you were blubbering to the God's of the sea for redemption. Who never let a man back on land without his due pay. That's old Mack, and you're robbing him. You might have well put a knife in my throat. That's what you did. A knife in the throat!"

When the soliloquy had ended, he sat on his haunches near the entrance to his hut. Mack seemed on the verge of tears as he continued to recite the damnation under his breath. I reached into my jacket and pulled out the remaining rye. When his eyes met the bottle, he looked as though presented with the image of Christ in all of his holy grace.

"Go ahead," I told him.

He had already started sucking it down. When there were

a few swigs left, he stopped, looking at me, through me.

"Let's go get another," he slurred

"A drink? I'm good, Mack. And you're stinko."

"What would you know about it?"

"Plenty."

"You were in Cathy's. You got money for love, but you ain't got anything for old Mack, huh?"

"Finish that up. We'll see about another. You still have your boat, a boat?"

"Ayuh, she floats. Or ain't you been listening, you poltroon?"

With that he got up, taking the empty bottle with him, adding it to his pile of belongings. He sacked out on his bed with his back to the room. I stood in the entryway looking down on him.

"You're right, Mack. I was in Cathy's, and I have been listening. I'm going out to the Naval Yard and, if all you're talking's true, then you're the only guy ready to be going out there anytime soon."

He didn't respond.

"Hank sent me down here to you, said you could be trusted. What does it take? Money, more hooch? I can get plenty of both."

"If you're wanting to be seeing the Yard so bad, why don't you cross the bridge. You newspapermen are always getting a special permit or greasing some wheel or some such."

"I'm no newsman and you're the wheel, Mack. I'm not passing any gate, and I don't care to be seen."

a three hour tour

I purchased my second bottle of the day from the clerk at the liquor store and got a look for it, but he took my money all the same. Mack waited for me on the corner. I handed him the bottle, and he began to drink without the desperation of before. He took nips off the bottle and, wiping his mouth, even offered it back to me. I accepted and took a gulp myself. My blood had stopped pumping after leaving Cathy's, and the pain in my face and side had started where the blood welled to bruising. The weather had worsened quickly and the bleak day had been whipped up with darker ink. The smell of grease or any other thing had been filtered away, and the air was brisk, carrying only the new rain fragrance of the clouds themselves. It would be even colder on the water, and I pined for a slicker like the one Mack wore, tattered as it was. We made our way through the center of town. Mack pointed.

"The gate to the Yard is there on that bridge. Any normal fella' would walk on or could drive on if he had permission. Unlucky for you the only other way in is from the Portsmouth side. They dock and service plenty of vessels and, in this weather, you might sneak in."

I gave the bottle back, and Mack continued to drink. We had come to the outskirts of the main street and started down toward the water, passing through a park, and glade of trees. There was a stone walkway here leading to a docking area filled with personal-sized crafts. Mack led the way down the path already slippery from the spray battering the rocks below. The wind blew in strong gusts, and the ships that were tied down had been lashed with extra rope to prevent shifting into one another during the storm. They seemed secure, so long as the dock didn't break up and float away. Mack went down on the dock and turned onto a floating extension. He stopped at a wooden dinghy with an off board motor and began to unstrap the ties that held it in place, bottle in hand all the time.

"This is your boat?"

I was hoping it wasn't.

"Ayuh. It's one of them."

"You don't have anything more, substantial?"

"You're the sneaky one. Would you rather go in a tugboat with a horn?"

Together we undid all the ropes but one at the bow.

"Now, go on in and crank the motor."

I got in. The whole thing rocked and shifted under me, but I managed to stay upright. I grasped the pull rope to the motor, threw the choke, and gave it a yank. There was a dull whine but no luck. I primed the gas a couple times and gave it another unsuccessful yank.

"Could the plugs be wet?"

77

Mack looked down on me, drinking, "No, they aren't wet. I could have started it twice by now if you needed me."

I went back to the starter without comment and tore at the rope several times in succession until a faint growl emerged from inside. I opened it up and touched the throttle, giving it juice.

"Okay, let's go if we're going," I said to Mack.

But he was already gone, asleep on the dock, bottle still in hand. I jumped up onto the dock and threw a spare rope around the rear end of the boat to keep it from drifting. Mack had passed out ass-backwards. The bottle, which still had a couple shots in it, had not left his hand. I took it from him and finished it off. I rolled Mack's weight over and took the slicker off him. The thing was huge on me, but the hood was in one piece and provided some relief from the onslaught of rain that was now soaking through my slacks. I covered Mack with a heavy tarp and got back into the boat. The engine was still running, and I unhooked the last two tie lines. It was immediately apparent that the going would be slow. Even here, by the dock, the waves were high enough to lift the propeller into the air at times. I began to cross toward the Naval Yard, cutting the waves as best I could without being turned over. I made the crossing in good time and was soon rocking up and down alongside the sheer cliffs that made up the island. There was no visible place to dock or even climb up. As the bay opened up, the waves grew in size, and I was riding upward on the precipitous water before reaching the crown and cruising back down to be encompassed by the swells, only to be swept back up again to new heights, leaning my weight back to keep the engine submerged. By the time I reached the immense barrier, I was completely soaked through and taking air in gasps. The boat had taken on water and was floating only inches from the surface of the sea. I maneuvered the rudder, going around the eastern wall of the dock yard at an angle so as to not be smashed sideways into the concrete. I rounded the corner and ended up in the docking yard. The Atlantic Ocean to my left, Naval Yard on my right, and though it couldn't be seen in the storm, there was a wall identical to the one at my back a few hundred yards in front of me. The two walls, tall as houses, jutted from the island, creating a north-facing cradle between the bay and the vast Atlantic. In this cradle the waves subsided to gentle rolling hills. A fog had settled above my head, making it nearly impossible to see more than a few feet in any direction. Keeping close to the wall, I took the boat in toward the island. The wind didn't blow so hard in here, and I could make out the sounds of chains and of the steel ship hulls which loomed up around me like canyons in the mist. The docks came up on me, and I cut the engine, allowing the waves to nudge me inland.

I tied the boat and climbed a ladder up to ground level. I stooped near a stack of wooden crates and peeked out from beneath my hood. I could hear the working sounds of a machine shop nearby and some voices shouting to each other. The rain had urged everyone inside, and I was free to move about in the immediate area. Jittery and cursing Donnie's name, I stepped out and walked across the paved roadway that separated me from the open garage bay doors of the machine shop. The roadway ran through several brick buildings resembling barracks and offices. Behind the machine shop was a hangar-shaped warehouse and then a much larger building with several smoking stacks coming from the roof. I cut down an alleyway and came to a double door that led inside the closest building. Keeping the slicker and the hood on, I ducked inside. The work floor was lit and filled with people working the pedals and levers of steel cutting machines. The noise of the machines drowned out all other noise in the room, and no one took notice of my entrance. I stayed close to the wall at my back and headed straight for a maintenance sign that hung near a stairwell. I took the stairs downward following the maintenance signs until the heat of the air changed and I was on the basement level. From the stairs, I followed a low rumbling sound down a hallway and soon came to the boiler room. I found a spot near the back of the room where I wouldn't be seen and removed the slicker. I took off my jacket and hung it next to some blackened brushes, doing my best not to get any soot on the fabric. I removed my bankroll and Nancy's envelope and laid those out flat on the floor near a burner. My matches and smokes I took out and laid on top of pipe overhead, which was hot to the touch but wouldn't burn anything. I stood there in between two burners for a few minutes letting the steam come off me. When my collar started to feel dry, I took down a smoke and a match from the pipe and gave them a try.

On my way out from the boiler room, I grabbed a blue denim jacket and similar hat that were hanging on a hook near the door. I put them on, instead of the beat-up slicker. I shoved my hands in the pockets of the denim and found a folded up pamphlet in one. The pamphlet seemed made for maintenance trainees. I opened it up and read a few lines about safety and security protocol and then found an itinerary in the back. This jacket belonged to a custodian in training. According to the itinerary, he was responsible for cleaning and performing general maintenance of the office and administrative buildings of the Yard. Unfortunately, according to my training documents, procedure was to check in, and check out keys for after-hours access to the buildings. It turns out I was a model employee and had turned in my keys at the end of my shift. I went back out the way I came, not running into anyone. Back outside, the garage bays of the machine shop had been closed against the winds. I headed toward the offices. A man wearing a denim jacket like mine with matching pants was leaving one of the buildings. I took out the pamphlet and slid a five dollar bill in the flap, so that it could be seen sticking out of the folded paper. I ran up to the guy and waved my hand.

"Excuse me, mister," I said as I approached.

"Yeah," he said.

"I was leaving for the day, and I think I dropped my keys in one of the offices."

"You don't say."

"I already started to change," I fingered the denim, "any chance you could let me back inside, let me search for them?"

"Where exactly do you think you dropped them?" he asked.

"I don't know. See, I unlocked the last few buildings on this block all at once. That way I could lock them up in order as I finished."

"That isn't really how we do things around here."

"I know. I was so caught up on getting done in time, I thought things would go quicker that way, you see?"

He eyed the pamphlet with the cash in it."

"Not really supposed to use our personal keys for things like that. Supposed to file a claim."

"I can't go filing a claim. If my wife finds out I got canned for losing keys, she'll wring my neck."

I extended the pamphlet with the fiver closer to him. He took the bill.

"I got an extra set I can turn in," he said, handing me a ring with several keys. "You give me these back tomorrow after you find yours. Which you better."

"You saved me, pal. I owe you."

"Yeah, you owe me those keys. I'll meet you right here in the morning."

"Sure thing."

He walked away, and I backtracked to the brick buildings closest to where I came in. On closer inspection, I saw the buildings were labeled above each door. I passed accounting, an executive office, shipping and receiving, admissions and discharge. I ducked into the admissions building, using the key. Once inside, I glanced back out the glass of the door. There was no one in sight, and I headed into the darkened first-floor bullpen fitted with a reception desk and several other personal office spaces with desks pushed together. Probably ten or fifteen people all worked in here together. Most of the desks had plain wooden chairs pulled up alongside them, chairs I had sat in, chairs for entrance and exit interviews. Guys sit there while their personal records are reviewed, waiting to hear whether they're too crazy for service or not crazy enough. Whether they get the rubber stamp marked 'fit for re-assimilation' or 'send him back'. Since the fighting was over, the 'send him back' option was no longer available, therefore, all the good old boys who landed in one piece or another were fit and healthy and ready for readmission to regular life. From pumping lead to pumping gas, from submarines to sub sandwiches, from corporal melee to creeping malaise, they came in by the boatload. The room ended in a stairway lobby. A sign told me that the archives area was in the basement.

I risked a light in the basement. There were stacks of shelves down here creating bound paper hallways through which I walked, glancing at the spines of record-keeping folders varying in size, all listed alphabetically. I slid a folder off a shelf to my right. It was labeled: Burnside. I had a ways to go. The wind could still be heard outside as I passed: E

The lights flickered. So far I had made a couple of turns going up and down the stacks but had already covered a lot of ground. If this basement was supposed to hold the entire base on file, it would be possible that this was a substructure that ran the length of several buildings above ground. I was sure that at this point I had crossed the boundary of the far wall in the rooms above me and must now be passing under the next office in the row of buildings by the time I made it to: H

I had certainly cracked a rib back at Cathy's. The pain in my head had moved to my jaw and the base of the skull: J

"Someone's been down here," said a voice.

It came from behind me. I regretted the lights.

"He was wanting to look for his keys, might be him," that was the custodian.

"I told you already, the new day-guy signed out an hour ago."

"Well, how the hell am I supposed to know that? There's new people passing in and out of here so often."

I took the denim jacket off and hung it up on the corner I had rounded. I soft shoed off in the other direction taking it easy but quick, passing: L

The lights flickered again.

"It's blowing something awful," the custodian.

By the sounds of it, they were still a ways away.

Lightning cracked outside. Thunder rumbled through everything. The rain had picked up again and could be heard pummeling the asphalt even from down here.

"There's the jacket he was wearing."

The lightning again. The thunder again. The ceiling lights dimmed, then intensified.

"He's gotta be close."

I could hear the footsteps now striding with confidence.

I had my hand on the folder: *MacRury, Martin G. LT.*

The thunder drowned out the footsteps. The lights flickered and went out. The thunder stopped, their footsteps stopped. The basement was silent. I carried on with MacRury's folder under my arm.

"Do you hear anything?" one of the guys whispered.

The other replied, but too low to hear. I was already nearing the end of the stacks, using one hand to guide myself along.

I found a concrete wall and from there inched forward until I caught something in the shin. I bent down and felt the wood slat of a step. I stayed close to the wall, making my way to the top soundlessly. I could hear the faint shuffling of feet down among the shelves but couldn't judge the distance. I made it to the top of the steps and found a door. I tried the knob, it turned. I swung the door open and lightning flashed through the windows.

"There he goes!"

I ran to the exit and threw the door open, then doubled back, heading upstairs. I stopped on a landing as the custodian and a guy who I could now see was a security guard burst out from the basement and ran through the open door and outside. The lights were still out, but a security bulb on the landing shined dimly. I took out the file and began flipping through. There were enlistment forms, pages of commemorations, of service records including assignment on the Tirante. There was more, health records and things like that. I found what I wanted at the end of the folder: MacRury's record of discharge. The door opened downstairs. I put the discharge slip in my pocket and went up the stairs.

"He could be anywhere," said the security guard.

"Everything's buttoned up tight," the custodian replied.

"He's got keys."

"He's in here somewhere," the custodian.

"I'll check around. You go upstairs," said the guard.

They made noises in different directions, and I went further up the stairs. This level was arranged with more desks. The walls between the buildings had doorways cut into them for crossing the entire top floor of the structure freely. I went toward the admissions building, where I had started. I opened the top drawer of a desk and stuck the folder inside. I could hear the custodian at the top of the steps as I passed into the next room. A door opened downstairs. The security guard was right on track with me, one floor down.

"Who's there?" hollered the custodian.

I didn't respond, and kept moving between the desks. I could hear the custodian following behind. I hugged the wall and took out the discharge slip. I neared a window on the side of the room and held the slip up, reading what I could: Date of birth, name, home address, training facility. Below that in a typewritten field for 'Engagement' a story had been written explaining the how and why of MacRury's excusal from service, but I couldn't read it. A portion of the text had been redacted. A door opened downstairs. I pocketed the slip, moving away from the window. The custodian had crept close to this room, and I quickly realized that I was faced with the stairs leading down to the admissions building where the security guard would be waiting. I turned to face the custodian and reached for my pack of smokes, tapping one out. The custodian came into the room as I lit up.

He approached me without getting too close.

"Hey there, pal," I told him. "I never did find my keys." I reached into my pocket and tossed his keys to him. He fumbled in the dark but caught them.

"Well, thanks for the help, pal. I gotta get home. The last bus passes by any minute now."

I waved to him and began to turn around for the stairs. I was never hit, didn't hurt at all. My blood got warm and a spot in my shoulder got real cool, and when the darkness came I was lost in it, except for the glowing orange tip of my cigarette shining in front of my nose like a sun which didn't pass any horizon as it set, but flipped stern over bow, tracing orange curls in the nothingness I was falling into.

The words on the discharge slip appeared, taking up my entire line of vision. The black ink of the typewriter swelled. The redaction bars warbled and dissipated, revealing questionable ethics in service, insubordination, racketeering. MacRury was on the Tirante. MacRury had a pearl grip automatic, sure as sure, probably issued by the captain or some Naval authority as additional recognition of the president's honor. MacRury was stationed in Kittery, but Amesbury wasn't all that far. His picture had made it that far: why not himself? Lights of unnamed colors darted through the centers of where I thought I was looking. I followed the shifting geometric colors without moving. I recognized the vibrant hues and, allowed them to become part of me, the need to breathe became unimportant. As I was filled with the pallet of color of what I realized was all things, tonality was washed away, and the whole scene was blown out so that I had to shield my eyes, which could not see, with hands that were not there. I was overcome with sickening fear. I closed my eyes, gritting my teeth against extinction, reaching out to hold on to any last-ditch thing.

The constraints on my body allowed only a slight movement of my extremities. I could move my eyes in my head, but it wasn't pleasurable and made me think of the colors and where they would take me if they came back. I had sweat through my shirt, and pants, and socks, pissed myself.

Dimethyltryptamine. DMT. Psycho-hallucinogenics injected

directly into the bloodstream: mind manipulation courtesy of the U.S. Navy. Another gem picked up from chemistry books of captured German scientists? Who knows what kind of torture tactics or super soldiers our top men have been developing with the stuff. I didn't have any point of reference, and the more tightly I tried to clench onto reality, the more it slipped away. The babel of nonexistent languages murmured in my ear that this time I had gone too far, I began to think that I had been given a heavy dose, and the voices unanimously agreed.

The door opened with a basement dankness that was fresh as roses in comparison to the rotten stench I had developed. In came a MP cadet with helmet and rifle. After him followed a man of about fifty. This one came in through the door in a way that, if it wasn't being held open for him, he would have smashed it down. He was Navy-dressed without a tie or jacket, sleeves rolled, shirt tucked, fancy belt. After him came another cadet, this one carrying a fire hose. He pointed the nozzle in my direction. We stayed like this for a moment, the cadet staring at me, me staring at the nozzle of the hose. The cadet by the door kept it open without moving. The older guy stood in the corner. Without command or any warning, the hose turned on. At least my shorts would be clean. The water stopped, and the cadet with the hose left the room. The one holding the door followed after and closed me in the room, alone with the older man. Water pooled on the floor before being sucked down a drain. The guy took out some things from his pockets and set them on a steel table on his side of the room. He looked over at me a couple times. One of the things he pulled out was a pack of smokes. They were mine, my matches, too. He lit one. The rest of the stuff he had laid out on the table was my bankroll, Nancy's envelope, the trainee pamphlet, and MacRury's folder. He came over to me and undid my hands from where they were bound, not taking the cigarette from his face. He left my feet secure. Then he got a smoke out from the pack and used his own burning end to light it. He rested the fresh one in my slackened jaw, and I sucked in. The smoke filled me up with a warmth and sudden sharpness of mind that comes to addicts each time they win their prize.

The guy watched me while I took the stick from my mouth and blew out. He went back to the table and grabbed a chair from the corner behind it. He put the chair in front of me and then went back for the table, which he wheeled over near me as well. Then he sat.

"Hell of a storm," he said, indicating the outside with his chin.

"Supposed to last days," I said.

"All the fisherman have shored up for the weekend so, yeah, I'd believe it." He was looking at me, smoking. I was smoking. We were talking about the weather. "You're a new hire, right? Starting today?"

"Yeah," I nodded.

"Oh, no, that's right, your name's Burke. You're the private detective hired from town."

"Right. That's me, Burke. Started here today. Private custodial services. Detecting all your trash, and rubbish too."

He put his cigarette out as he stood, and when I looked down, I could see that he had stubbed it out right on the back of my hand. The crushed cig stayed upright in my burnt flesh until I picked up my hand to inspect it. The guy stood at the table and opened up Nancy's envelope.

"Measly retainer you got out of her, though a guy who rolls around with a few hundred in cash doesn't need to be paid in advance, I guess."

"It's money to pay you off."

"No dice."

"Good, I need the dough anyway."

"I'd think you were nuts if I didn't know you were goofed. You aren't getting out of here any time soon. That dough belongs to the U.S. Navy now."

"So then it is still like I bribed you." I flexed my hand with the burn.

"Is that starting to sting?"

"Yeah."

He popped me, right in the teeth. The guy could hit, and I was receptive enough. I leaned over in the chair and picked up the half a cig he had knocked out of my mouth. I put it back. It still worked. He sat again and lit a fresh smoke. Then he fished something out of his shirt pocket. It was a piece of folded paper. As he undid the creases, I was able to see that it was the photo from Cathy's. He laid it out on his knee and flattened it with both hands.

"That's Martin MacRury in this picture. Good man, good sailor. You know that though, you've been looking him up."

He waited for something smart. I didn't give it to him.

"Obviously you know Captain Ford. Everyone knows that. One of the most highly decorated commanders we have around here, and rightly so too. You know anything about the word valor?"

"I could spell it."

He popped me again. This time the cigarette went clear across the room.

"You know plenty. I'll tell you something I know, too," he leaned into me. "I know where this photograph came from. I know the exact spot."

I let him keep looking at me.

"Catherine runs a top-notch house, and her girls provide an important service to the men of this base. I've heard talk over there in the barroom, about how Cathy blames him for crippling her. She should know all the good this base has done for her. During wartime she was living like Rockefeller off of those enlisted men. She wants to blame the Navy for ruining her marriage, I say blame the man."

I had no idea what he was talking about, but he seemed to like doing it so I let him keep going.

"They always say, don't mix love and business. Don't they say that?"

"I think they do."

"Well, they'd be right. I'm no great thinker, but I think this: Love will always outfox business, and pride will always cast a shadow over shame."

I was starting to drift, so he slapped me in the cheeks a couple times with his open mitts.

"You hearing me, Burke? I'm helping you investigate, isn't that what you're here for?"

He socked me. Blood from somewhere dripped on my

shirt. I watched as he tore the photograph of MacRury and dropped the pieces on the floor. He took the cash out of Nancy's envelope and tore the retainer up. He picked up my private license and driver's license, and held them together in his hand. Sitting again, he examined them.

"You should have stayed in Boston, Burke."

"No kidding."

He lit up another of my matches. He held up my licenses and, with the burning match, began to ignite the damp paper cards that burned slowly but surely. The flame crept upward, nearing the pertinent typed information.

"Just fine."

When the door burst open this time it was like all the air was sucked out of the room, taking the flame of the match with it. The singed corners of my licenses extinguished themselves in the guy's hand. He looked over his shoulder in agitation, but whoever it was that interrupted us hadn't come in yet. The guy set my licenses down on the table next to him, looking at the darkness beyond the open door.

"Lieutenant," a voice came from outside the room.

The lieutenant, stood, tossing the cigarette on the floor. He stepped outside the room, partially closing the door. There was a hushed conversation that I couldn't really make out. The lieutenant was obviously receiving orders and spoke only sparingly. The last thing I heard was a not completely resolute, "Yes, sir," and then footsteps. The lieutenant came back inside with a hangdog face. He stood by the door without coming too close. The two cadets came back into the room, one held the door wide open, the other came right up to me and knelt, undoing the restraints on my legs. The lieutenant grabbed my licenses and cash off the table and shoved the wad inside my jacket pocket. He turned his back on me without a word and walked out of the room. I felt a twinge in the back of my arm and my blood tingled and I was being carried by under the arms out of the chair and through the door. The drugs were taking over and I was in no position to fight it off. The second cadet closed the door behind us.

I was floating on my back past the walls of the hall that I knew were there because I could see the faces trapped behind them, pressing against the root and stone, hoping to emerge on the side of the living.

Then I was outside, and I knew it was real. I knew that the wind whipped at my face and the rain once more soaked my clothes. The whole sky around me was a dome comprised of a continuous series of geometrics. Then I was falling. The hands that carried me were gone, and I was on my back, undulating with the dinghy on the waves. The waves came up over the side of the boat now, but I wasn't moving. I didn't get up and bail the water, I didn't try to start the motor by furiously yanking the cord. When the boat had gone, it wasn't as though it had sank but more as if there never was a boat to begin with. The water passed around me as I cut through and, when I glanced back, I could see my mind in the tumbling wake. I felt the same great importance of escape, thrashing wildly to gain traction in the slippery molecules. The more I struggled, the heavier I became and, before long, was completely submerged. I recognized this place. I moved forward, without legs, deeper into the inconceivable depth. I reached with arms that were not there. If only I could be faced once more with the light. I would withstand the brilliance of it this time and, as the walls that surrounded me now would fall away, so would I. The light did not come, and as I sank the colors swirled around me, to which I gave no resistance.

I felt the warmth of another hand on mine, then another, yanking me upward and over a ladder on the side of a fishing boat which had fared better than Mack's dinghy. And there on the slick wooden planks among the lobster traps and chum, I found my salvation as the fingers of my savior compressed my rib cage, forcing the salt water from my gut. He rolled me onto my side, pumping my arm, and more saltwater syphoned out of my mouth until finally I could breath again.

The drugs were wearing off for the second time as the boat fought through the bay. The captain, a man twice my age with short graying hair, released his vice grip on the helm only when the sand of the shore came up under us. The man climbed out onto land and threw a tarp over most of the boat. I wanted to get up and help as he began to tie and spike straps over the top of the boat, but the radio static in my head was still faintly denying me certain physical capacities. It wasn't until he had secured the boat and unloaded his catch and ice chests that he returned for me. By this time, I had gotten my head up over my knees, and he gave me a slicker which I wrapped around myself and then clumsily helped him strap down the last piece of tarp.

It wasn't long before we were in the center of town and I

could see the Naval Yard beyond Cathy's house. There was no sign of commotion or intrusion. Like I was never there. When we reached Hank's, the guy stopped and shut off the truck.

Some of the mess around Hank's chair and the fireplace had been cleaned up, and the fire had been kept. Hank wasn't in the room. I started to take off my wet jacket and shoes. The man pulled one of Hank's chairs up to the fireplace and put me in it. From the other room—the kitchen—there was the sound of cabinets closing and then Hank.

"Who's that in there?"

"It's me," the man replied.

"Wilson?" Hank called back.

"You know it. Hank, come on in here. We got a city boy that damn near about drowned out in the current."

"Place is lousy with guys from the city. Earlier today I–" Hank stopped when he came in the room. "You crazy sonofabitch, look'it this guy."

He meant me.

"Hey, remember me?"

I nodded.

"Yeah, I found him sinking like a stone," said Wilson.

"This guy's all right. Name's Burke."

"He isn't going to be right much longer. He's getting purpler."

"Wrap him in some dry towels. Not too close to the fire. Warm him up slow. You're gonna be all right, Burke. We'll take care of you."

"How you know him, anyway?"

"He's a private dick, like I was."

Wilson looked at me different then. I can't say for better or worse. He went out of the room, leaving me there with Hank, who looked much better than I last saw him. He put a hand on my shoulder.

"I'd say you found Mack by the way you look."

"Yeah. I found him."

"He tell you what you needed to know, or what?"

"Nah. Gave me his boat though. It sank."

Hank gave me a curious look and then started for the lobby.

"I got what you need."

As he walked out, Wilson came back in carrying towels and blanket, had me take my slacks off, then handed me a towel.

"Shorts too. They silk?"

"Why, you need a pair?"

He threw the blanket over and around me.

I sat again and wrapped my feet in the towels. Hank came back in the room with a tray. On it he had, a kettle, some mugs, a bottle of rye, and a pack of smokes.

"What is this, my last meal?"

"It's because of you I went and got this. When you left here, I woke up feeling so good I figured I better have the stuff on hand. Who knew I'd be using it again so soon."

"You not feeling well, Hank?" said Wilson.

"I wasn't 'til I met this guy."

"What are we drinking?" Wilson wanted to know.

"Jeez, I don't know."

"Toddy," I told him.

"I'd be fine with the rye," said Wilson.

"Nurts to that," Hank replied. "You probably need it as bad as him or me. Besides, I made the whole batch, I'm not wasting it."

"All right, don't get yourself worked up. But pour it strong."

Hank poured the whiskey into mugs. Then he added the steaming tea mixture. Immediately the familiar smell of herbs and citrus filled the room. I managed to keep the cup upright and held it in both hands until I could feel the faint burning of the ceramic in my palms. I sipped, and it was strong, doled out by Hank's heavy hand. I shot a look at Wilson who had tasted it, and he looked right back at me with an expression that I would guess said, I only wanted the whiskey.

The current in the bay between Kittery and Portsmouth is the strongest in the region by far. Getting caught up in the undertow at unawares is the closest thing you'll get to a death sentence without a hangman. That's what Wilson told me anyway and Hank confirmed: third-strongest in the world, he had heard. I sat with my two friends, filling our cups with booze as the tea was drunk. Hank pulled out a smoke and offered me and Wilson the same.

"I can cover you for the tea and the smokes and everything. You, too, Wilson. Don't think I don't owe you."

"How do you two boys know each other? You don't sound like a New Yorker."

"I'm not," I told Wilson.

"Joe happened through yesterday. He's an old friend of Mack's," Hank explained.

"Givens?"

"Yeah," Hank turned to me, "you didn't really say what happened when you found him."

"I found him down at Cathy's, like you said. Brawling with

some friends. Catherine had enough I guess, 'cause she chased us out. I was gonna ride across the bay with Mack to the Yard, but he tied one on too fast for me, and I went alone."

I smoked, breathed out heavily, and looked between the two men waiting for me to speak again, which neither of them did.

"I didn't mean anything about Mack passing out. I've had my runs as a drunk before, there's no shame in it."

That wasn't it. It wasn't anger or distaste that made them quiet. It was something I recognized but couldn't associate with these two hardened men before me. It was fear that shut them up, and it was fear in their eyes that locked on me as I glanced between them. It was Hank who spoke.

"You called her Catherine."

hold fast

The storm had picked up even worse and Hank had switched on a couple lamps. Wilson had poured more booze into our cups and lit his own smoke. I got sick of being looked at, so I threw a log in the fire and touched my slacks, which were still damp.

"You here working for Marty?"

"No."

"Cathy?"

"No," I told Hank again.

"You went to Cathy's though, yeah?"

"I did. I met Mack there, like I said."

"No one in there called her Catherine, though, did they."

"Not that I heard."

"So where'd you hear it?"

"Out in the Yard with those Navy boys," Wilson broke in.

"That's right. Some lieutenant got the same idea you have. Started telling me all about MacRury and how Catherine should leave him alone."

"And that doesn't mean anything to you?" Hank continued.

"Not squat."

They looked at each other.

"What did he do to her?"

"He left her, that's for sure," said Hank.

"What was he doing in Amesbury?"

"What makes you think he was in Amesbury?"

"Because I was there. Down there, his picture's on the wall. That same picture is now hanging behind Cathy's bar."

Wilson stood up.

"Thanks for the drink, Hank. I best be getting back before Becky starts to worry."

"Let me pay you for your trouble," I said.

"No thanks. As far as I care, I've never even seen you."

"See ya, Will," Hank said, standing up.

He sat again, fresh smoke, more booze. The fire made patterns on our faces.

"You're into something sticky, Joe."

"Tell me about it."

"I'm telling you. What were you doing in Amesbury?" He leaned in.

"Got hired for a gig. What's with the line of questioning?"

"What gig?"

"Personal matter. A kid looking for her brother."

"You were in Amesbury looking for some kid's brother, and she tells you the best place to start would be the Yard?"

"Every hick town has its dirt. How the hell am I supposed to keep straight whose it is on my shoes?"

"I spent a lot of time in the city. Got so I had a life there.

Had my own routine, got to know a few people. But all the people in a city, rushing all around, yapping their heads off, looking for their break, you don't really get to know anyone all that much, if you get what I mean. It gets so you go days without even seeing a guy you think you know. Then you see him, and you get to wondering, what was he really doing those last few days? Where had he been? Then you consider that you've never even been inside his apartment or met his folks. Moreover, you get to thinking how you never seen his license or been to see him at work. Soon you're wondering about where this guy is really from and if it's Winnipeg, like he said. And then before you know it, you never see the guy again. I don't know if he was a good guy or a bad guy. Did he give his kids the belt? Did he go ballroom dancing on Friday's? Did he drive around with a half rotted body in his trunk?" Hank flicked the dead cigarette in his hands and lighted it again. "And that's the thing. I'd never really know. Now come back here. Look'it Wilson. I know him, seen his I.D. and name printed right in the cabin of his boat. I've been to his house, put the dishes away with his wife Becky. Know they had a son that died, drowned right out there in the bay. I was at the boy's funeral. And Will and Becky, they were here taking care of my old man when he was no good. And they were there with me when he died."

We drank.

"You heard about the trials in Amesbury? A woman named Mason, put away for killing her husband?"

"Yeah, I seen it. Her and some other kid."

"Bingo. That kid's my kid's lost brother."

"No fooling?"

"Not at all."

"So you really don't know MacRury or Cathy?"

"Like I said."

"So what, you came up here for the dough?"

"Initially, but there hasn't been much of it to go around."

"Then why don't you tell me what you're doing here now?"

So I did. I told him about Nancy's phone call and my time in Amesbury, Hansen and his boys, Charlie and Dale, the pearl-grip automatic, the letters from Donnie, the photo of MacRury in Nancy's apartment, all the way up until it came to us sitting there with Wilson earlier. Hank listened intently. When I was finished, he waited to make sure before he stood and added another log to the fire. He felt my slacks and my jacket and then started taking them down from where they were hung. He returned to the table and put them in front of me. He sat and dumped the final mouthfuls of whiskey into our cups.

"It's a shame about that kid Nancy," he said finally.

"That's what I'm trying to figure out, how to help her."

"You're asking for directions back to Beantown."

"What are you talking about?"

"You know what I'm saying, Joe."

"Hank, I'm trying to help this girl. I'm paying out of pocket. I've about been killed every day this week, and so far you're the only person it seems actually has the sense to give me an idea of what I'm into around here."

"Get dressed. I'll give you a lift back to your ride."

I got the wad out and started counting bills.

"This is for you, for taking care of me. But give me some information. You can do it, you'd be helping a lot of people… helping me."

Hank put one hand over both of mine and stopped me counting the money. He looked at me like a father looks at a son when his dog has been hit by a car. Maybe he really understood how desperate Nancy was, how desperate I was.

"It's like you says, Joe. You don't know whose dirt you got on your shoes."

The mile markers passed quickly, and soon I was out of Maine. When I finally saw a sign telling me where I was it said Exeter, eight miles. It wasn't the direction I was headed, but it still wasn't too late, and the druggist might still be open. I pulled off where the sign said and found the drug store easy enough. A light was on in the store. I found the druggist wrapping up for the night. He turned to the door smiling, but his expression changed when he saw who it was.

"It's you," he said.

"Evening there, sir," I said happily.

"How was the funeral?" he nipped his words.

"As good as a thing like that can be."

"You must have missed your photos."

"Sorry about rushing you and never picking them up."

"No bother."

We stood there for a minute. I spread my hands at my sides. After he felt he had stared at me for a sufficient amount of time, he retrieved a package from under his counter and walked it over to me, pushing it into my chest.

"Here's your pictures, what came out. There's your money back, too."

He was right, the cash was folded up inside the package with the developed pictures. He began to walk away.

"I'm sorry I didn't make it back on time, but I'd still like to pay you."

He turned.

"Keep your ill-gotten, filth money!"

"Scuse' me?"

"We don't deal in smut around here."

He pushed me, and I was so surprised I stumbled right back. I continued to back away and went right out the door, which he slammed and locked from the inside. I was making friends backward, and fast. I took the package back to the Chevy and stood with the door open. Most of the photos had come out either black or very blurry. Some, though, had come out and, when I saw them, I understood the druggist's anger. There were pictures of several people at a time, sometimes with others in the background. Sometimes it was people having laughs and lying around. Sometimes it was people stripped down to their altogether and going to town on each other in what some might consider a rather offensive way. Some were racier than others, but they all painted the same overall image. By the time I got to the end, there were a few faces among them that I could recognize. Elizabeth Mason was there. MacRury was there. Donnie appeared in the images sparingly, having been the one taking them. When he did appear, it was usually nude, up close with one or more of his close friends or with Elizabeth, with MacRury, with MacRury and another man.

There was a lot of trading back and forth and a lot of group activity. After a while, I got to a point where I wasn't seeing anything new—and then I did. It was Donnie again, the dope. He was nude, right up against a blonde-haired girl about his age. He held onto this one especially tight and, in a couple of the photos, they kissed passionately. In the last photo, Donnie and the girl looked right at the camera, their naked bodies side by side. The girl had changed, but enough was the same: The blonde hair wasn't much of a cover, and if anyone who knew her then saw her now, they'd probably know her as the same. I got into the Chevy and closed the door, turning around and doubling back faster than I had came, pushing the Chevy for more than it was worth and grumbling at the nonsense whine of the engine, whirring in top gear and threatening to bust and pushing it more. There were some people in the photos I recognized and some I didn't. The girl in the picture with Donnie had changed, but I knew her the same.

I tore into Nancy's neighborhood and stopped at a line of parked cars about half a block long. I gathered up the photos and pulled out some selects, the ones with faces that appeared more than once. The rest I wrapped back up in the packaging. I grabbed the .38, which was still strapped in its place. It came with a holster that snapped onto my belt. My jacket covered the whole thing. I opened the trunk and used my pen knife to slit a pocket in a seam of the interior. I slid the package inside, under the lining of the upholstery, and pressed the cloth back into the crease to hide my work. I started toward the house and, from a distance, could already see the lighted windows and hear the tinkling music. I went up the front steps and put my hand on the knob. As I did, the door opened inward. I was greeted by a man and woman in formal attire, the woman with some black feathers and diamonds. They were talking over their shoulders as they left. Behind them the lively party was in full swing.

"Hey, there!" said the man when he almost ran into me.

"Excuse my husband," said the woman, putting a hand on the front of my shoulder.

"Excuse you," I said, removing it.

"Sad sack," said the husband.

They both laughed and brushed by me, out the door, holding onto each other for dear life. I closed the door and ventured further, past more of the same well-dressed types, sitting, reclining, drinking. A dance floor had been established, and when the three-piece band picked up a waltz, couples stepped along. I noticed two women dancing closely, not minding the pace, arms draped over each other.

"Drink?" came a voice from behind me.

A server with a tray offered champagne. I ignored him and walked past the dance floor to the grand stairway. In an alcove with a phone near the bottom landing, a group was gathered, giggling and sipping. There was music on the upper levels as well, but it varied and came from speakers in seemingly separate rooms. I could see down onto the party from here, and my presence hadn't interrupted a thing. All the doors up here were closed, and I approached the one closest to me from which was coming rather loud jazzy music. I cracked the door that opened onto a reddish darkness in which I could make out the figures of ten or twelve people, all with their backs to the door, some alone, others in pairs or even groups. Hands reached over shoulders, fingers caressed necks, bow ties were loosened, but the greatest attention was paid to the couple in the front of the room, furthest from the door. I couldn't make out faces but it was clearly a man and woman, both naked, the woman on her hand and knees, the man holding her from behind. Their voices were drowned out by the music, but their mouths formed and reshaped the expressions of passionate and expletive language that didn't need to be heard. I closed the door and moved on, checking on the other upstairs rooms, I found more of the same, some shows like before, others more private, but all occupied for the same purpose. The last door, a double door facing the stairway opened onto a kind of library converted into a lounge with cushy circular benches and booths. There were perhaps more people in this one room than in the rest of the house so far. Clothed and unclothed, they wandered around, talking quietly, drinking in sips, covering their mouths, and pointing with their eyes. On the benches, on the floor, bent over a desk, were men and women, women and women, men and men, and other equations to be made from such, in various stages of the amorous act of public love-making. I took in the scene and listened to the inane snippets of conversation that passed by my ear, as if the only things separating tonight from dinner and drinks at the Jones' was the geography. I hung near the wall and lit up, feeling out of place and getting sidelong glances thrown at me by the majority of those in the room. A couple set up shop on a chair very close to me and, being only human, I took a good look. They had attracted attention, and a crowd had formed.

The door opened, and a young guy entered. He wore all black, gloves and hat as well, which was a contrast to his very light if not pale skin. Beneath the hat some very blonde hair could be seen sticking out over his collar at the back. He closed the door behind him, adjusting his gloves. He had a sallow face that had spent too much time at a desk and a tight mouth which he kept balled up in the bottom of his face. It wasn't hard to see from here that one cheek was raised and purple, and the man adjusted his hat in a self conscious effort to distract from the welt he knew was so obvious. He looked in my direction, and I didn't look away. He immediately turned and went out.

I left the room and closed the door behind me. The young stranger had begun making his way down the steps and turned to look back as he went. I started down after him and was cut off at the bottom of the steps by a gang of well-dressed but intimidating gentlemen. A door opened upstairs, and the mob appeared at the top landing. I kept going forward, breaking through the crowd below, and saw the young stranger go out the front door and close it behind him. I cut across the main hall. A couple of guys stepped out to the head of the crowd, readying their knuckles. I opened the front door, and found Nancy standing on the other side.

"Mr. Burke," she said, "I was beginning to worry."

Over my shoulder, the crowd was at bay. A few lingered, staring, but most broke off and went back to the party. I stepped outside. I could see the stranger walking away in the distance. He got into a black Cadillac and drove away. I stepped after him, but Nancy barred my way.

"Mr. Burke."

I moved past her, walking across the front yard, stopping between the main house and the driveway leading to Nancy's. The Cadillac was gone. Behind me, the lights of the house shone bright and yellow, passed by shadows of the people I had seen. I could still hear them at times, but outside it was quiet, too early for the night noises to have started.

"This is all over, kid," I said.

"Mr. Burke. Won't you talk to me?"

"What do you want to talk about, Nance?"

"I don't know. I haven't seen you for two days."

"I've been busy. What were you doing here?"

She made an uncomfortable laughing noise.

"You know what I mean. Why did you come to the door?"

"I was going to ask if they could please keep it down. This happens almost once a week."

"You know what's going on in there?"

"I always assumed it was rented out for society meetings or something like that."

"Never even been inside?"

"No."

"Did Donnie hang around here at all?"

"No. Why don't we go inside."

"But he could have been hanging around here. You wouldn't know though, 'cause you hadn't seen him in a long time before the trial, isn't that right?"

"I'm certain he wouldn't is all I meant."

"Very certain?"

"Certain."

I slid out fifty bucks from my wad and stuffed it in her palm.
"What's this?"

"Your retainer."

I took the photo of Nancy and Donnie out and handed it
to her. The muscles of her face were calm, but her skin turned
white, and then green, and she dropped the photo.

I turned away from her and walked the rest of the way
through the lawn, darkening the toes of my shoes in the
moist grass.

"Joe," she practically screamed, tears in her eyes and falling
from her cheeks. She grabbed at me. I held her by the wrists.

"Get away from me, kid. I ain't got time."

"But, Donnie–"

I took the rest of the photo selections from my jacket. One
by one I showed them to Nancy, crumpling the corners in
my clenched hand.

"What about Donnie? About Elizabeth, and Martin, and
Cathy, and Cliff Mason, and who else? Who else, Nancy? Half
the town, and you too."

"I was so scared, Joe."

I picked up a couple of photos that had fallen.

"I'm sorry," She sobbed.

I didn't respond.

"Didn't you hear me? I said I'm sorry."

"Yeah, I heard you."

She fell to the ground, sitting back side-saddle on her heels.
The door to the house opened, and several inquiring minds
jostled for the position of most interested and ready to do
something about it.

"You've known all along who owns this place and what goes on here, haven't you? Are you even Donnie's sister?"

I'm not Nancy Brighton, okay. There never was one. My name is Rebecca Miller."

"Like Wainsforth, Miller? I know it's garbage, kid, so why not come clean? Who are you really, Ford's dame on the side? Was Cliff getting fed up with his wife hanging around here? Was he about to get too loud about the private lives of all your best customers."

"You don't even know."

"You couldn't let him bring the roof down on the swinger's ball, so you killed him, you and Ford, and pinned it on Elizabeth. But Donnie knew too much, and he had the hots for Elizabeth, so you had to find him next."

"No, he did not!"

The crying stopped. She was scarlet with anger but it didn't faze me.

"And how would you know? Are you secretly Elizabeth Mason as well?"

"No."

"Well, who the hell are you kid? I don't know why it matters. I'd like to know before I go."

"Judith Whitlock."

I was sure I hadn't heard.

la maison derrière

"My name is, Judith Whitlock," she repeated.

That one hit me hard. I hadn't even stopped to think about it, the woman Donnie was colluding with the night of Cliff Mason's murder, the woman whose testimony was sworn into court, though she herself never appeared. A woman whose very existence was questioned by the greater New England area and provides the only plausible alibi for Donnie Brighton was crying at my feet in the grass. The bystanders had grown in number under the front house light.

"Everything okay down there, guy?" a bold one called out.

"Sure thing, pal," I told him. "Go back inside."

"What's that?" He stepped forward.

I did the same, flashing the piece on my belt.

"You got potatoes in your ears? I said back inside."

The main crowd retreated, spurred by the reproach of their fearless leader, whom I could hear asking why no one had stood up with him.

"Come on, Nance," I stooped. "Or should I call you Judy?

Either way, on your feet, kid."

She had stopped most of her bawling. I put my arm around her, and she shambled along with me toward her apartment.

"I loved him, Joe. I really did."

"I bet he loved you, too, kid."

"No, he didn't. It was all a game to him. We all loved him, and he only loved himself."

We were at the door now, going into the back house. The sound of some car engines starting up could be heard.

"What about MacRury? Martin MacRury, did he love Donnie?"

"Sure. He probably did, I don't know."

"More than he loved Catherine?"

She was breaking down again. I could see the tears running down her cheeks.

"But Donnie couldn't be held down. Is that what you're telling me? Is that why MacRury is trying to find him? Is that why you dragged me up here?"

"Poor Martin," was what she said. "Such a good man, and he was always hurt so badly. By her and now by him and then."

"How did Donnie hurt Martin?"

"Not Donnie, you muddle-brained clod!"

"If not Donnie than who? What happened to MacRury that made him want to find Donnie? Would make him kill for it? Did MacRury kill Cliff Mason?"

There was a noise, glass breaking, hammer and flint. Combustion. Propulsion. Did she deserve what she got while she stood there with me in the room with her clothes on the ground? She continued to search for answers to questions that I had given up asking, and soon she would too. She slumped into my arms. Wet meat. Footsteps gained distance from the broken window outside the cottage, back toward the road. A commotion was in the air, and cars started up much more quickly than before. I laid her on the bed and pressed on her stomach near the bottom of her ribs where the bullet had gone in. Her breath was short, going in and out in gasps. Punctured lung probably.

"You're gonna be all right, Judith."

She wasn't.

"You know my name's not even Judith. It's what he told me to call myself. For the papers."

She coughed blood.

I pressed harder on the wound, brushed back the hair from her eyes.

"Did Elizabeth kill Cliff Mason?"

She shook her head, no.

"MacRury?"

Again, no.

"Talk to me, kid. Was it Donnie? Is it Elizabeth who hired you to get me to find him?"

She couldn't talk. The blood was coming up in spurts now. She reached for a nearby picture and smeared it with blood. I held some of the pictures up to her and she pointed, straining to move her arm. I held out the blood-smeared image, and she pointed, not at the picture but to the left. I moved the photo, trying to help her level her finger, but each time she moved it to the left, off the frame, pointing at nothing. I had probably already lost her. She struggled to lift her head and spit out the blood that had filled her mouth. I leaned in close to her and she put her lips to my ear, leaving faint traces of the red stuff each time she moved her mouth. I felt her breath as she whispered, and then the warmth of her as she kissed the side of my face, and then she was gone. I stood up, grabbing together all of the photos that had been strewn about. No sooner did I pocket the pictures than the front door burst open. There stood Hansen in all his glory, backed by Duffy and Richardson. Their guns were drawn. The reds and blues shone on their backs, casting intermittent flashes on the body behind me.

"Easy does it, Burke. You keep your hands where I can see them," Hansen spoke.

"Oh, Jesus Christ, is she dead?" Richardson sounded panicked.

"Keep your shirt on, rook," Duffy told him.

But he didn't. The rook retched and put his hands on his knees. Hansen didn't look too impressed.

"Look, Burke. I don't know what the hell's going on here, but why don't you come down to the station and explain. I've shown you twice now that I'm a reasonable man."

"Okay, Captain," I said.

He lowered the aim of his weapon.

"You gonna listen to me now?"

"Sure thing, Captain."

But I didn't. I went for the window in the closest wall. It was a cheap wood-paned job, and the bullet had already broken most of the frame. I lunged for it and ate glass, landing hard on the sod. I was on my feet before taking a breath and in the tree line headed for the road. A couple shots rang out. The bullets whizzed by the back of my neck, striking the thick tree trunks behind me.

"Cease fire!" I heard Hansen shouting.

The commotion had really picked up, and people were flooding to their cars in groups, some still half-dressed, panicked by the gunshots. I blended in with the crowds, going for the furthest parked cars looking for the Chevy. It wasn't hard to spot.

Some of the party had gathered around, others still passing by straining their necks to see. The whole thing was engulfed in flames. Fire wrapped around the roof where the windows had been. Black smoke curled into the air. The front tire burst. I pushed my way through the crowd and grabbed a blanket off of a shirtless guy who was using it to cover up. He came at me, but I took the .38 off my belt and pushed it toward him. The onlookers dispersed, and he went with them. I wrapped my hand in the blanket and popped the trunk. The interior was already burning, and the photos under the upholstery had singed but were still intact. I backed away from the car, and in the fire's glow examined the images for damage. I took out the blood-smeared photo I had shown Nancy and looked closely. She was right: the upper-left-hand corner of the frame showed a man's shoe and pant leg. I flipped through the stack of burnt images, all of the close-ups. He wasn't a foreground character, that's why I didn't notice him, but when I held the burnt photo up to the its blood-smeared companion, they created an overlapping panoramic view. The pictures must have been taken from a slightly different angle almost instantaneously. A mistake by the novice photog borrowing Donnie's camera? The place where Nancy had pointed was a man I should have recognized. The man was Admiral Ford. He was having a conversation, but the man's eyes were fixed on the blood-smeared image. He was watching Donnie pose for a rare photo of himself alongside MacRury, both smiling wide, their hands gripping each other's sides.

I felt the movement behind me and crouched, but the Cadillac Kid still got me good with a crowbar right in the shoulder. I slumped over, and he grabbed for the photos, knocking them to the ground. I swung at him, punching him in his already swollen face. He lunged at me, knocking us into the burning Chevy. My sleeve caught fire, and as I was pulling my jacket off, the Kid went for the crowbar again. He swung it into my side, catching my arm stuck in the jacket. I pulled the .38, but he knocked it out of my hand, so I grabbed his arm and twisted until it snapped. I took the crowbar from him and hit him in the leg above the knee. He faltered and began to crumble. As he went down, I swung again from above, landing a blow on his shoulder below the neck. He hit the ground. I checked him for a piece and found a recently fired pistol. I dismantled the thing and left it in the road. The photos were on the ground where they fell, and my jacket wasn't burnt to a crisp. I put it on and folded the pictures, pocketing them. I found the .38 and holstered it. There was a sound of footsteps on the road and then, Hansen.

"Freeze, police!" He stopped, aiming his gun.

I ducked, hidden behind the next car over from the Chevy, but he wasn't talking to me. The Kid was on his feet, pointing a revolver he must have had hidden somewhere. The Kid meant business and got the hammer on the thing all the way back before Hansen shot him. The Kid hit the ground, and I crept away, staying low behind the row of vehicles while making my way up the street. Hansen gave orders to Duffy and Richardson, who went off back toward the house. I moved when I could, staying under cover. When I made it to the end of the line of cars, I waited near the driver's door of an older model sedan. Hansen was on the other side of the street checking that row of cars. The window to the sedan was open, and I reached up into the sunscreen for the keys, not there.

"Hey, Captain!" Duffy ran up to Hansen.

Hansen didn't respond. He kept looking all around the cars.

"Captain?" Duffy again.

I opened the driver's door soundlessly and slid into the seat, keeping my head down. Hansen began to walk back toward Duffy, motioning for him to quiet down. I took out my pen knife and used it to cut out the wires from the starter. I connected them, and the engine turned over. I put the transmission in gear and slammed the door. I could see in the mirror that Hansen had turned, but he didn't give chase or fire a shot.

"Go home," Nancy had said to me. I wiped her blood off my ear and the side of my face. Among the vehicle owner's possessions I found a half a book of matches, a pint of scotch left over from the owner's party planning, a clean undershirt, and some smokes. I drank the scotch in mouthfuls, letting it sit and tasting it. I splashed some of the stuff on my forearm, where the fire had burned through and charred the skin. I fished out a smoke and lit up. MacRury hadn't killed Cliff. Donnie hadn't killed Cliff. Even Elizabeth, in jail for the crime, didn't actually commit it. It was the man not in the picture. The man whose name I can't tell you, says the girl with three names and maybe more. Whispered with her blood.

I was out of Nancy's neighborhood and back into downtown Amesbury. The police hadn't followed so far, and the streets were devoid of any sign of the gathering that had dispersed only blocks away. I got into Plum Island before the only bar in town had closed and parked across the street. I could see the bartender at his post wiping the mahogany. There were still a few patrons tying the last of one on, a young guy flirting with his date, a couple barflies I recognized from days earlier. I had to burn a few of the smokes before it was finally time for everyone to clear out. When they did, the bartender began his closing ritual, and I crossed the street. The door was still unlocked. I stepped right in.

"Closed, mister," he said, without looking.

"Charlie stopped by lately?"

The bartender was still bruised from the beating Charlie had given him.

"Get the hell outta' here." His voice was a high-pitched whine.

"What about, Martin MacRury? He stop by lately?"

Only the distance of the bar separated us now.

His eyes darted down.

"Got a piece under there," I asked.

The punk pulled a shotgun from under the bar. He swung the barrel around to get it level. I grabbed in mid-swing and it went off, hot fire in my hands. Bottles on the wall shattered.

I took the gun from him and used the butt on his forehead. He hit the ground. I reached over the bar, felt a box of shells, and pocketed a handful. Keeping the unfired barrel on the bartender, I walked out of the bar and back toward the Dodge. I got in and sat.

After a minute or two, the bartender got up on his feet. He went to the front door and peered outside. The Dodge blended right in. He locked the door without noticing me watching him and went for the back room where he kept the phone. I started up and drove off further out onto Plum Island, past the one-story shacks boarded up with driftwood. It wasn't long before I was on Charlie's street.

The neighborhood was quiet. It was late, but in Charlie's there was still one light on. I stuck a fresh shell in the empty chamber of the shotgun and took it under my jacket, creeping around the back of Charlie's place. The ocean was coming in. I climbed up the dumpster and slid the shotgun onto Charlie's back porch overhead. The water sucked the sand back with it behind me, raking the surface. I climbed up and over the porch, taking the long heater in one hand. The curtains to the sliding glass door were closed from the inside so that I couldn't see anything but their plain backing. I pressed my free hand against the glass. When the waves advanced again, I slid the door deftly aside, not disturbing the curtain. The ocean drew back, and I could hear inside. It was quiet. If Charlie was home he was sleeping or listening, like me, to sounds of the waves.

I shouldered the cannon and stood. Using the barrel, I brushed the curtain aside. The waves broke again. I could see into the room. There was a chair turned to the front door. There was a television and radio but nothing on. The bed would be in the wall somewhere. A formica counter top separated the two sides of the one-room apartment, living area and kitchen area. There was a high-caliber revolver on the counter and next to that a short novel opened face down and a half glass of beer. I had the curtain almost all the way open. I was about to step inside when I heard the sound of running water. A door opened in the right hand wall. Charlie stepped out of the bathroom. Where he stood, he was about the same distance from the gun on the counter as he was from me.

"Hey, there, Charlie."

He didn't respond. The waves came in. Charlie looked at the gun on the counter and then at me. He took not quite a step toward the counter. The barrels followed his movement. He stopped.

"Judith Whitlock is dead," I told him. His mouth worked slightly, but he still didn't speak. "That means something to you. Your buddy with the pale face who drives the Caddy, him too."

"You're probably gonna tell me next that you're the fella who killed Dale." He rubbed his neck.

"This town of yours seems to be taking care of things all on it's own."

"Not my town, bub."

"Who killed Cliff Mason?"

"His wife."

"We must read the same papers."

"You're in over your head." He took a step toward the bar, and I moved past the door frame.

"How do you know Admiral Wayne Ford?"

"I don't."

"You know who he is, though."

Charlie shrugged.

"You ever spend any time at the house in Amesbury? You know which one."

"Other than the time looking for you? Not once."

"But you know what goes on there? Admiral Ford owns the Amesbury house. He owns Cathy's place in Kittery, too."

I took Charlie's silence as an affirmative.

"Ford served with Martin MacRury. Spent something like two years in a sub together. MacRury was married to Cathy before that, and when he came home, she noticed something had changed. It wasn't long after that, MacRury left Kittery and left Cathy behind."

"You get paid for this?"

"Ford owned the Amesbury house already. MacRury had learned the business from Cathy. They were a match made in heaven, and they were in love, but was MacRury in love with Elizabeth as well? They certainly had the chance to be intimate. Is that why Ford killed Cliff?"

"Tough stuff, Burke. It must be rough to be so close to something but really have no idea."

"Listen to reason, Charlie. You've barely done anything wrong. There's an innocent woman in jail. An innocent man on the run. What did the Cadillac Kid have on you? He's dead. Half of everybody that matters in the whole thing is dead. What have you got to lose?"

"I had an okay thing going here, dick."

"You still can, Charlie. Help me out. Where's Ford?"

He looked at the gun on the counter again. Looked at his hands. Then he looked at me, or past me where waves were still going about their monotonous duty. He charged me. I'd have killed him dead a this range with the shotgun and swung it at an angle, pulling the trigger before he reached me. The spread winged him but didn't slow him down. He took me by the gut and into the porch railing, which gave way under us. We hit the sand below, and Charlie's weight came down on me, knocking the wind from my lungs. I got to my knees, leaning on my hands. Charlie was on his feet and grabbed me by the back of my collar, dragging me to the surf. I grabbed at the sand and put my hands on the shotgun that had fallen nearby. I swung the thing by the barrel hitting Charlie with the stock, right in the ribs, where I'd shot him. He doubled over, and I stood, slinging the shotgun around his neck, me now dragging him. I backed into the icy water and pulled him under. A wave submerged his head. I held him down there, His arms reached up around my throat, but he couldn't get any grip. The ocean pulled out around my feet revealing Charlie to the cold night air. His hands went to the shotgun. He sucked wind.

The rollers broke hard from above us, and I almost was pushed under. I dug my shoes into the wet earth up to my ankles and held Charlie down. When the sea receded again, he was still. He choked quietly, not struggling. I bent down and dragged him to the dry sand. He got himself together, and I helped him to his feet. I put the barrels on him and patted him down, ankles and all.

"Stick your hands in your pockets." He did. I nudged him. "Walk." We walked out toward the street. It was dark on the block, and no one was around to notice us. I directed Charlie to the Dodge and opened the driver door. "Get in." He did. I went around the other side and got in. I laid the shotgun across my lap practically touching Charlie's ribs with the killing end. I kept my right hand on the trigger. I reached over Charlie with my left and put the wires together, starting up the engine. "Let's go see Ford."

"You don't even know what you're talking about."

I pressed the shotgun into Charlie's bleeding ribs.

"I'll take you where you want to go. Some stubborn bastard you are."

"Drive."

I unholstered the .38 and emptied the wet cartridges. I wiped the whole thing down inside and out before putting it back together. I opened up the rye from the bar and drank from it. I handed the bottle to Charlie, and he drank from it a few times before passing it back. I lit a couple of smokes and gave him one.

Charlie was silent on the car ride. He kept his hands on the wheel, eyes on the road. I broke the shotgun and stuck it in the back. The shells in the breach and the extras in my pocket had swollen in the ocean. I might have killed us both if I had pulled the trigger on the thing and besides, the .38 was enough to keep Charlie calm the rest of the way. The open flesh under his flannel shirt must have been burning but, if it was bothering him, I couldn't tell. By the time we hit Maine, the sun was rising, unabashed by cloud or haze.

I found myself on familiar streets. We were heading back to Kittery, back to the Naval Yard. The storm had subsided more quickly than the old fishermen had assumed and the whole place had a shiny newness to it that comes after rain on bright days in cold weather. Charlie drove down the main street, past Hank's and the general store. He came to the road leading to the Naval Yard and passed it. Then he found a turn off and parked there. We were in front of Cathy's house. The shutters were closed tight. Leaves stuck to the boards of the porch and filled the lawn on either side of the walkway leading to Cathy's front door.

"We're here?"

Charlie nodded.

I stepped out of the passenger's side keeping the .38 at my hip, "Get out." Charlie got out, and we closed the doors., "Ford's in there?"

Charlie wasn't really the question-answering type.

"Just fine." I let Charlie lead the way up the front steps. When he got to the door, he stopped and waited. He turned his head slightly to look at me, and I nodded. He opened the heavy front door. The sweet smell of the place greeted us, and I shut the door against the brisk outdoors. It was quiet in the house. We walked through the empty foyer into the empty parlor. Upstairs, a bottle clinked against a glass. A stool moved on the floor boards followed by footsteps. Charlie and I stood in the center of the room, him a couple steps ahead of me, me with the .38 still at my hip. Cathy appeared at the top of steps and looked down on us. She wasn't dressed in the exposing garters and lusty accents that she wore the other day. She had on sleeping pants and a blouse, her hair down, letting out the last of its curl. In her one hand, a glass tumbler from which she drank dark booze. In her other, a pearl-gripped automatic Navy-issue pistol. She finished the booze and she threw the glass, shattering it on the steps. The automatic hung loose in her hand, but her finger remained on the trigger at all times. She descended the stairs one by one, crushing the shards of glass with her slippered feet. When she reached the base of the steps, she stopped, Charlie between me and her. She raised the automatic and it went off twice, shooting Charlie in the chest. He collapsed on the ground at my feet. Blood came fast, pooling around him. He was dead.

"Hey there, Cathy,"

"Hey there yourself, Mr. Burke."

She shot me. It must not have exited 'cause I could feel it in my gut. The blood started seeping into my waistband. I stepped back, losing my vision momentarily. I found myself a chair and sat down. I pressed on my stomach with my left hand, which brought on the pain. I rested the .38 on the table at my side.

"Where's Ford?"

"Upstairs." Her eyes found the door with the gold plaque on the second floor.

"That's his pistol or MacRury's'?"

"His."

"You used it to kill Dale, too?"

"Not me, sugar. Ford used it, like he used it to kill you. Right before I killed him in self defense."

"Nancy's dead. Judith. Rebecca." She hadn't known that. "Was she one of your girls? Yeah, I think she was. Until Ford took her away from you, like he took MacRury." The lady already shot you once, Burke. Do you have to egg her on?

"She was a good girl once. She had a way about her that didn't fit in around here . I say good riddance."

"Where's Donnie Brighton?"

"That weaselly kid? I don't know what they all saw in him."

"He was blackmailing all of them. The Masons, too. Half the town probably. He had pictures."

I reached inside my jacket and pulled out the folded photos. I tossed them on the table.

"Ford should have never got you involved."

"Judith pretended to be Donnie's sister. Said he went missing."

Cathy sneered, turning her gaze up the steps to the second floor.

"Always getting everything all twisted, that's like him."

"Ford took Judith from you, took your husband, but it was MacRury's idea to start hosting at the Amesbury house."

"Why did he leave me?" she was looking at the images on the table.

"Because they were in love."

"That wasn't love." She turned on me. "That was that damn Navy, that damned ship, driving them together, away from me."

"When they started the Amesbury house together, Ford and MacRury, you didn't try to stop them?"

"That little swingers club?" she looked disdainfully down at the photos. "A bunch of bumpkins swapping wives. I'm running a corporation, Mr. Burke. I've served the hearts and minds of thousands of men through this port. Let them have their parties."

"I didn't think that bothered you much. And you would have let Ford go right on with business as usual if he hadn't started stirring the pot, searching for Donnie."

"I wondered why Cliff Mason wasn't in any of the photos." I held up the image of Ford. "I thought Ford was to blame. Did anyone else know that MacRury was Cliff Mason?"

The disbelief was in her eyes. "He never could leave well enough alone."

"Elizabeth had already confessed, but you threatened her next, threatened the kids? Was that the worst thing, knowing they had children together?"

The pain was gone from my stomach. My whole lower half was getting cold.

"He said he would never love another woman," if she could cry, she was doing it now. "He needed a man. I thought I understood."

I held up the picture of MacRury and Donnie. She took it from me. She was shaking.

"Did anyone besides Ford know that MacRury changed his name?"

She shook her head no.

"Not even Elizabeth?"

"No," she said.

The bleeding from my gut had slowed but hadn't stopped. She stared at the photo, at MacRury. We had gotten everything out in the open, even if we were the only ones to know the whole story. She raised the automatic, the pearl grip shining under her palm. She never took her eyes off the picture. I pulled the trigger four or five times. I had to leave the .38 on the table to keep it steady. A couple shots missed, but the ones that mattered landed. She fired once, but it went high, then the gun fell from her hand. When she hit the floor, the photo was still clutched to her chest.

the bridge out of town

Hansen sat in a chair smoking the short end of a cigar that had been lit several times before. He wore his shirt sleeves and suspenders, his jacket and shirt draped over the chair behind him. He had spoken to his wife and told her not to wait up and to kiss the kids for him and to wrap up the brisket for tomorrow when he'd be home. Duffy had brought him a couple of sandwiches and the newspaper and fresh underclothes, and even a couple of beers. He had waited there in the chair for the better part of a week. He was the first thing I saw when I opened my eyes from the hospital bed.

"Cathy's dead?" I asked.

"She is."

"What about Ford?"

"He's being held back at the station. We found him tied up in a room at Cathy's. Looked like he'd been there a couple days."

"Elizabeth Mason didn't kill her husband."

"That's what he says. They tell me he's blubbering and talking up a storm, no lawyer or nothing."

"Martin MacRury was Cliff Mason. Elizabeth never even knew. Cathy killed him for a lot of reasons, and killed a lot more to cover it up."

"I'll have to send someone in to get a full statement from you. After that you'll be free to go."

"What about Cathy?"

"The way it looks is, you stopped a killer. The D.A. isn't interested in pressing charges, I don't think. He's got enough to deal with covering his ass reopening the Mason case and making up reasons why his Assistant D.A. murdered that Whitlock girl."

"The Cadillac Kid?"

"Yeah. Way I see it is, whatever Ford's talking about that Brighton had on him, he had the same thing on the D.A., too. No one wants their private business all out in the open. Who knows how far a person's willing to go to stop something like that."

"Far."

"This stuff belongs to you." He handed me a yellow envelope and a pack of smokes. "I got the smokes for you."

"Thanks."

I opened the pack to light one and found my hand, cuffed to the hospital bed rail. Hansen rose, unlocking the clasp.

"You made a hell of a mess, Burke. But it's for the best I imagine."

I got a smoke out. Hansen lit it for me.

"They said you aren't supposed to," he told me.

I could feel the pain in my gut as I drew in.

"She got you good I guess. You'll stay here and take bed rest another day or two if you know what's good for you. Which I don't think you do."

"Are we in Amesbury?"

"You'd better believe it."

"You had me followed?"

"A cruiser picked you up coming from Exeter the other night, driving like a tick into a dog's ear. They were with you after the D.A.'s boy got it, and at the bar, and on Plum Island too, all the way up to Kittery."

"Why didn't you haul me in?"

"Lot's of reasons. Could be I thought you were onto something, could be I thought better to let you get yourself killed, or it's like you said and it had something to do with how I sleep at night. Speaking of which, I could use ten or twelve hours, and Mrs. Hansen's probably had all of the boys she can handle on her own. Take the doctor's orders, stay here a couple days, get some rest."

He placed his palm on my shoulder before turning to go.

"Swing on by the precinct before you go on your way, I'll give you a hell of a deal on a ride home."

I drove up the seacoast. Olfactory details riddled the summer day—honeysuckle and cut grass, felled lumber and sod, manure, oak, apples. The Cadillac handled like a dream: velour interior, leather wheel and dash, wood grained detailing, hydramatic transmission, the works. Hansen had sold it to me for a cool fifty bucks out of impound, which seemed fitting. I left Amesbury before any of the juicy stuff really got into motion, but I'm sure the town would have plenty to talk about from here on out. Ford was being held in protective custody, for his own good in case some loose end should appear before he could testify in court on the new facts at hand. Elizabeth Mason was released from prison on probation and was staying in a nearby shelter run by nuns. She was allowed to see her children and for all intents and purposes was a free woman. The D.A. had ensured her a clean slate plus reparations, condemning the Navy, the legal system, the townships of the seacoast, and mostly everybody except himself in the matter and made such a spectacle of the joyous event of Elizabeth's freedom that it was almost enough to forget his own dalliances, though no one did. Repealing the charges against Elizabeth and beginning a very lackadaisical, though semi-honorable, investigation into the local Navy Yard would be the last of his notable measures in public office, and he resigned from his position within the year. I found the used car lot in Seabrook and the salesman gave the old Buick back to me, plus double the price he paid in cash, in exchange for the Cadillac and I was on my way. The Buick felt like new, and it was good to be behind the wheel. The thing had been cleaned and buffed, and the bomber-sight hood emblem stood at straight attention guiding the way back through Amesbury and over Deer Island on the bridge crossing the Merrimack.

this world, then...

"I'm stopping by the bank and then I'm going home. Don't forget you have an appointment with Mrs. Abernacle at nine in the morning. I'll be here to open up. Are you leaving soon?"

Vicky stood at my desk wearing her purse over one shoulder. She had put down the necessary dough to hold onto the office while I was on vacation in Amesbury, held my landlord at bay, too. I tried to pay her back, but she wouldn't hear of it. She made herself partner instead, said she spent more time in this office than I did so she might as well be invested.

"Yeah, I am."

"You really should. Why don't you walk? It's a beautiful day, you can get a car tomorrow if you need to."

She forced a smile.

"Goodnight, Joe. I'll see you at home."

She went out the front and turned the lights off in the ante-room on her way. The sun hung around late in the day, cutting through the blinds, radiating in the smoke of the room, making patterns on the walls and on my hands. I finished the rye in the glass and poured another. I flicked the stick in my hand and ash fell on the wrinkled picture spread out on the desk. I had found it folded up at the bottom of the yellow envelope. Hansen must have pilfered it out of evidence and stuck it in there for me to find. A close-up, two faces taut with happiness. Nancy, Judith at the time, side by side with Donnie, their bare shoulders touching. Had Donnie known where she had come from? Did he figure out to get well enough away? Is that the sun setting on the horizon or a reflection in the sea.

"Go home," she said to me.

I wonder what she said to him.